HEATH'S CHOICE

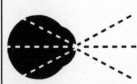

This Large Print Book carries the
Seal of Approval of N.A.V.H.

KENTUCKY WEDDINGS, BOOK 2

HEATH'S CHOICE

TERRY FOWLER

THORNDIKE PRESS
A part of Gale, Cengage Learning

Detroit • New York • San Francisco • New Haven, Conn • Waterville, Maine • London

GALE
CENGAGE Learning®

Copyright © 2009 by Terry Fowler.
Kentucky Weddings Series #2.
Scripture taken from the HOLY BIBLE, NEW INTERNATIONAL VERSION®.
NIV®. Copyright © 1973, 1978, 1984 by International Bible Society.
Used by permission of Zondervan. All rights reserved.
Thorndike Press, a part of Gale, Cengage Learning.

Thorndike Press® Large Print Christian Fiction.
The text of this Large Print edition is unabridged.
Other aspects of the book may vary from the original edition.
Set in 16 pt. Plantin.

LIBRARY OF CONGRESS CATALOGING-IN-PUBLICATION DATA

Fowler, Terry (Terry S.)
  Heath's choice / by Terry Fowler.
    p. cm. — (Thorndike Press large print Christian fiction)
  (Kentucky weddings series ; #2)
  ISBN-13: 978-1-4104-4482-0 (hardcover)
  ISBN-10: 1-4104-4482-1 (hardcover)
  1. Life change events—Fiction. 2. First loves—Fiction. 3. Man-woman relationships—Fiction. 4. Kentucky—Fiction. 5. Domestic fiction. 6. Large type books. I. Title.
PS3556.O86H43 2012
813'.54—dc23   2011053012

Published in 2012 by arrangement with Barbour Publishing, Inc.

Printed in the United States of America
1 2 3 4 5 6 7 16 15 14 13 12

To my brothers Billy, Steve, and Tim. Love you guys.

And to those forced to live with the choices made by loved ones. May they feel God's healing love.

ONE

"You remember Jane Kendrick from high school?"

His older sister's voice faded into the distance as Heath Truelove stared into the beautiful green gaze he'd found so mesmerizing in his youth. If possible, Jane Kendrick Holt looked more beautiful today than she had in high school.

She flashed the appealing smile that had first attracted him to her. *She hasn't changed,* Heath thought. "Sure do," he said as he moved to stand. "It's good to see you."

"You, too." Jane waved him back into the booth and when he slid over, sat down next to him. "Val keeps me current on you guys. Congratulations on your degree. How's Rom?"

Heath swallowed hard and said, "Thanks. He's good. We're waiting for him now. He had an interview today."

A frown touched her beautiful face. "Hope

his luck is better than mine. I should have accepted that clerk position."

"No, you shouldn't have," Val said. "I have a couple of ideas that will work for you in the future. You deserve better than a minimum wage job."

"Now is my future," Jane said unhappily. "I have to find work."

"You will. Join us for lunch."

"Yes, please do," his younger sister, Opie, said.

"I don't want to intrude."

"You know us Trueloves. The more the merrier," Opie said with a big grin.

Jane accepted and ordered diet soda. Heath sat back and watched the interplay between her and his sisters. Obviously she and Val had formed a close friendship. Heath wondered when that had happened.

"Why don't you come out to the farm tomorrow? I have an idea I'd like to discuss with you," Val said.

"Can I bring Sammy? I called in the last of my favors for the interview today."

"Please do. Daddy might even take her for a ride."

"She'd love that. She's so horse crazy right now."

"Who's Sammy?" he asked.

"My two-year-old."

8

"You have a daughter?" Jane's nod reminded him she was off-limits — another man's wife. "I know Garrett is very happy."

Jane's ivory skin paled even more before she said, "Garrett's dead, Heath."

His heart took a nosedive into his stomach. "Oh man, I'm sorry. I didn't know. What happened?"

The words were out before he caught his sisters' warning headshakes.

"He killed himself," Jane said, her voice breaking.

The revelation stunned Heath. Why hadn't anyone told him? He talked to his family regularly, and no one had said a word. It couldn't have been that long ago. Last time he saw them, they were living and working in Lexington after Garrett dropped out of the University of Kentucky. He had visited the coffee shop now and then while he waited for Rom. He'd enjoyed watching Jane with the customers. Her friendly personality made her popular with the patrons.

"Wouldn't you love to see a picture of Jane's daughter, Heath?" Under the table, Opie's foot connected painfully with his leg.

He jumped and said, "Sure. Is she as pretty as her mom?"

Heath noticed the way Jane's cheeks

flushed with the question. He appreciated his sister's attempt to salvage the situation. He'd blundered big-time. He should have just waited and let it come out naturally.

"She's beautiful." She dug around in her huge purse and pulled out a brag book. "But that's a very prejudiced mom talking."

As he viewed the photos, Heath had the feeling that little Sammy looked very much as her mother had as a child. "You're entitled. She's gorgeous," he said, handing the photo book back to Jane.

"She makes my life worth living."

"I can see why."

"I've spoiled her terribly," Jane admitted. "She can be quite a handful."

Their group continued to grow as they waited for Rom. Russ Hunter, the architect who Val had hired to design a structure for Your Wedding Place, showed up at the restaurant, and when he stopped to speak to Val, Opie invited him to join them. They asked for a larger table, and Rom joined them a few minutes later.

Just as Heath expected, Jane fit right into the group. She caught up with Rom, who somehow managed to avoid the topic of Garrett's death. When Russ brought up the subject of the seven Truelove kids' nick-names, she chuckled and said, "I still remember the first time I heard them called by their real names. We had a substitute, and she was checking attendance. When she said Heathcliff and Romeo Truelove, I couldn't believe they were really named that."

"Jane is a name from the classics, too," Heath said.

She made a face. "Jane is a grandmother's name. Not romantic or fancy. Just plain Jane."

The conversation moved on to Val's project and other topics, and Heath found himself following Jane's responses. She laughed, joked, and stayed right in the middle of everything, just as she'd done all those years ago. All too soon lunch was over, and the group started to break up. Russ made his excuses and returned to work.

"I need to pick up Sammy," Jane said. "It's been great seeing everyone again."

"You, too," Heath said, standing when she pushed her chair back. "I'm really sorry about Garrett."

Jane smiled sadly. "Thanks."

"Please come to the farm tomorrow," Val said. "I really want to talk to you."

"Sure," Jane said. "Just name a time. I have a serious gaping hole in my schedule at present."

"Come around eleven and stay for lunch."

"You don't have to keep feeding me," Jane protested with a smile.

"I'll make one of my culinary specialties," Opie offered.

Jane nodded. "We'll be there, though I warn you Sammy's a picky eater."

"Ah, but she's never had an Opie Truelove meal."

"Is that like a fast food kid's meal?" Val teased.

Opie grimaced at her sister and then said, "Once she tastes my food, you'll have problems getting her to eat anything else."

Jane laughed and said, "I'll risk it. Thanks for lunch."

"Don't thank us," Val said. "Russ Hunter paid."

"Thank him for me when you see him again."

She waved bye as she walked toward the door. Heath's gaze never left her.

Jane unlocked her truck and climbed inside. She had needed this. Limited conversation with a two-year-old made those times she was in the presence of adults even more special. She had enjoyed the lively interaction of the five adults and the challenge of keeping up with the discussion.

Yet another reason she missed her job at the coffee shop. She'd enjoyed catching up with the people who came in for their daily coffee runs.

Jane wondered what Val wanted to talk to her about as she drove out of the parking lot. The need to find work had become a necessity, but Jane couldn't imagine what Val thought she could do to help. Then again, Val had the money to do whatever she wanted. Maybe she planned to open a coffee shop. Jane still couldn't get over the fact that her best friend had won millions with a lottery ticket gifted to her by her boss.

Val had shared a number of her plans, including the purchase of Sheridan Farm where her father had worked as a manager for the previous owner, and then her plans for Your Wedding Place had struck Jane as a total fantasy with a healthy dose of financial reality. Her friend planned to utilize twenty-five acres of the farm, including the spectacular existing gardens and the house to create venues for brides who wanted unusual wedding locations.

Jane had no doubt the Trueloves would utilize their money to help others as well. She'd witnessed Val's huge heart many times since they had struck up a friendship. And she remembered Heath and Rom from high school. Everyone in their class knew the two kindhearted, intelligent young men would go far.

She had enjoyed seeing Heath and Rom. Like everyone else, the twins fascinated her, but today as she looked at them, each so alike and so different, she saw men who stood on their own. Jane didn't know why she'd never realized how attractive Heath was. His strong, clean-shaven facial features and neatly trimmed dark hair said a lot about his need for a clean-cut personal appearance. He'd worn well-pressed khakis and a long-sleeved baby blue oxford shirt that lay open at the neck.

Jane found his personality to be his best feature. He could laugh at himself, didn't mock people, and obviously loved his family. She had always considered him serious minded and more mature than his years, and yet today he'd been right in his element with his sisters and brother teasing him. If anyone fit the family man image, it would be Heath. The way he laughed with easy abandon fascinated her. It had never been something she associated with his more serious nature.

The Trueloves had an interesting family dynamic. She wondered if the others had noticed the change in Val when Opie invited

Russ Hunter to join them. The two sisters had lingered behind when they had changed tables, and Jane didn't think Val had been too happy about the situation. His references to making progress on her project seemed to strike a dissonant chord as well. Perhaps they were at odds over the work.

She signaled and turned into her friend's driveway. She'd visit for a while and then take Sammy home. At least she had something to look forward to tomorrow. Maybe even plans for the future, and she couldn't think of anything she'd like more.

TWO

Early the next morning Heath lay in bed, thoughts of the reunion with Jane filling his head. Awakened by the younger boys' school preparations, he hadn't been able to go back to sleep. His mind reeled with the news of Garrett's death. "Hey Rom, you awake?"

His twin grunted from the lower bunk of the beds on the opposite side of the room and pulled the covers over his head. The four of them had shared the room with two sets of bunk beds since the two younger boys had moved out of cribs.

He crossed his arms behind his head and said, "Jane looked good, don't you think?"

Rom grunted again.

"She's coming out this morning to talk to Val about a job."

Rom thrust the covers aside, pushed his legs over the side of the bed, and sat up as much as the lower bunk would allow. "Yeah,

I heard."

"She looks good."

"Yeah. I heard you the first time." Rom rubbed his face. "You always said she was out of your league."

Heath exhaled noisily and said, "I know, but I felt like I'd been poleaxed yesterday when she looked at me and smiled."

"She's still a looker," Rom agreed.

Heath knew what Rom was thinking. His twin had seen through his efforts to hide his attraction back when he was a boy of fourteen and Jane had entered their freshman class in Paris, Kentucky. He still remembered the first day she showed up at school.

She gained everyone's attention when she walked into the classroom, her waist-length blond hair swaying as she flashed the liveliest smile and whitest teeth he'd ever seen. She sat one row over from him and always seemed to have something going on.

Jane wore her hair short now, but though it was as blond as it had been then, he didn't think the color came from a bottle. Petite and thin, she didn't look like she had a two-year-old child.

For years he had admired her from afar. The cheerleader and most popular girl in their class had been nice to him, but he had known he didn't stand a chance of getting a date with her. Particularly after she'd become involved with the football quarterback, Garrett Holt. Then in their senior year she and Garrett had married hastily. That summer, rumor had it their baby had been stillborn. That fall, Jane and Garrett had moved into married student housing at the University of Kentucky. Occasionally he saw them on campus, but he and Rom had driven from Paris to Lexington and lived at home, so he hadn't seen them often after graduation.

"Always has been. You know how I felt."

"I know you said you didn't stand a chance," Rom said. "What makes you think differently now?"

"I'm not thinking differently," Heath said somewhat defensively. "I'm just saying it was good to see her."

"Oh, you're thinking," Rom said without doubt.

"I'm praying that God will send the right woman, but so far that's not happened either."

"You think she's the one? Did you hope that Jane would become available again?"

Heath shot up out of the bed. "No way. I was shocked when she said Garrett was dead. How did you manage to avoid the subject?"

Rom stopped rummaging through the dresser drawer and looked at him. "You didn't know?"

"No. I can't believe no one said anything. I felt like a blundering idiot."

"I thought I told you," Rom said thoughtfully.

Heath shook his head. "No one in the family said a word. Not even Val and she attended the funeral."

"They probably thought you'd seen it in those local papers they sent us in Boston."

"I definitely missed the obit. What if seeing her again is a sign?"

Rom pulled on a T-shirt and asked, "Do you want it to be?"

Heath considered the question.

"You know how she was in school," Rom said when Heath didn't say anything. "Do you believe she's changed?"

"I know what was said, but I never believed Jane's reputation was as bad as gossip made it sound."

Rom's skeptical expression showed he lacked his twin's opinion of Jane. "I don't know, Heath."

Determined to put her in a better light, he said, "Think about it, Rom. She only dated Garrett. Then she married and stayed with him. Don't you think he would have dumped her if the rumors were true?"

"Who are you trying to convince?"

He shrugged. "I doubt it matters anymore now than it did then. I'm not Jane's type. She likes the more athletic type."

"Don't sell yourself short. You have a lot to offer a woman."

"Yeah, a couple of college degrees really go a long way when it comes to attracting a woman."

"Don't put yourself down like that. You'll be a much better provider because of those degrees."

Heath pushed down the guilt that spiraled through him at the dread of taking an office job. These last few days had been a reprieve from the responsibility he knew he had to shoulder. "Guess I'd better get started if I plan to finish those trees today."

"I'd help, but I promised Dad I'd give him a hand."

"I've got it under control." Heath grabbed his robe and headed for the shower.

"Heath," Rom called as he neared the door. "I'm praying, too. You'll find the right woman."

Jane awakened early that morning, her head filled with the myriad of worries that weighed her down lately. She sat at the table, enjoying the diversion of the two squirrels that chased each other in the small yard as she drank her coffee.

Her eyes dropped to the bank statement on the tabletop. The minute savings account she'd managed to hold onto was dwindling fast. The rent on the little house she'd lived in for the past three years was paid until the end of June. After that, she had no idea where she and her child would lay their heads. That frightened her most of all. She didn't want Val Truelove doing anything out of charity, but if it was a legitimate job offer, she had no choice but to accept.

The mother in her instinctively recognized the sounds of stirring that came from Sammy's bedroom. Pushing open the door, she took a moment's pleasure in the room she'd decorated so lovingly when she learned her child was on the way. Once she became pregnant, Jane had insisted that they find a house. Apartments with no lawns weren't what she wanted for her child.

" 'Morning, sweetheart," she cooed as she lifted Samantha and gave her a hug. "We're going to see the horsies today."

"Horsies?"

Jane carried Sammy over to the changing table and quickly changed her and dressed her. Sammy wasn't as cooperative when it came to the socks and sneakers and curled her toes.

Jane drew a finger along the sole of her foot, and Sammy giggled. Her daughter was very ticklish. "We're going to see Mommy's friends who have horsies."

"Fends? Me see horsies."

Taking advantage of Sammy's distraction, Jane worked the tiny foot into the shoe and pulled the Velcro tab into place. She lifted and swung her around, enjoying her laughter. "Yes, sweetness. Let's get you fed and go meet Mommy's friends."

When Heath saw Jane's truck drive up, he put the chain saw aside and walked over to greet them.

"Hi," Jane said, smiling at him before she opened the back door and leaned in to unhook Sammy. The child all but bounced out of the car seat.

"Well, hello there, cutie," he said to the little girl. "I'm Heath. Can you say Heath?"

Sammy rewarded him with a smile and stretched out her arms to him. "Want Hef hold me."

"May I?" he asked.

Jane let go when Sammy bounced impatiently, all but diving into his arms. "What is it?" he asked when he noticed Jane's widened eyes and wrinkled forehead.

"She never goes to strange men like that."

"I'm not strange," Heath protested with a grin. "Am I, Sammy?"

The little girl patted his cheeks with her tiny hands. "Hef have horsies? See horsies?"

"No, you're not," Jane said, embarrassed by her words. "I just meant . . . Garrett would get upset because she cried when he would take her."

"Me see horsies?"

He chuckled. "Somebody has a one-track mind. Think she'll stay with me while you go in and see Val?"

Jane hesitated. It would help her discussion with Val go more smoothly. She'd wondered how she would keep Sammy quiet long enough for them to talk. Leaving her with Heath seemed like the perfect solution, but Sammy had no idea who this strange man was. "I don't know, Heath. She can be a handful."

"What if I promise to bring her to you if she starts to cry? Otherwise we'll stay right here in the garden and play. You'll be able to see us from Val's office. All right, Sammy?"

The child clapped her hands together. "Sammy see horsies."

Jane relented. "Thank you."

He flashed a smile and said, "Val's waiting in the office. Go in the front door. First room on your left."

Jane watched as he stood the toddler on her feet in the grass. Sammy immediately took off, and Heath easily captured her. Jane laughed at his "Whoa there, little miss" when he pulled her back by the tail of her shirt. His soft tone as he talked to the little girl filled her heart with longing. Jane had dreamed of Sammy having this type of relationship with her father, but Garrett had destroyed any hope of that happening.

Pain spiraled through her. She couldn't think about that now. Jane hurried inside. It wouldn't be good for her to take advantage of Heath for too long. Inside the mansion, she stared in awe of the beautiful surroundings. What would it be like to own such a home?

"I thought I heard the door," Val said as she stepped into the hallway. "Quite a place, isn't it?"

"Incredible." Jane allowed her gaze to shift about the room. "I had no idea."

"I lived on Sheridan Farm all my life, but the big house was off-limits. Now that it's ours, we're all adjusting to the changes. Where's Sammy?" she asked.

"In the garden with Heath."

Val nodded. "Come into the office."

Jane listened while Val outlined the position duties. She couldn't help but feel as if it was too good to be true.

"It's not anything you're used to," Val said. "Daddy might send you into town to pick up a part. Mom could send you to the grocery store. You'll be helping in the gardens. Later, you'll assist with bookings and site preparation for the weddings."

"And you really intend to hire an assistant?" Jane asked. "I mean . . . well, I don't want you feeling like you have to help me."

"If it's not you, it will be someone else," Val said. "I've seen you in action at the coffee shop and think your experience would be a bonus for us both. It's not going to be easy. I'd expect you to work as hard as we do, but I'd pay you a fair wage. Later, as the plans develop, you would be considered for any managerial position that comes open if you're interested."

"When would I start?"

"Whenever you want. Tomorrow is good."

Why couldn't she just put aside her doubts and accept the opportunity she was being handed? "Can I think about it and get back to you later?"

Val flashed a sympathetic smile. "Don't

think too long, Jane. You said you need to work, and I'm offering you a job. I have great plans for my business, and I'd like to have you with me. If you're concerned about it being a new business, let me assure you I have sufficient funds set aside to accomplish my goals. I'm not planning to change my mind and leave you unemployed again."

Jane couldn't dispute that she needed to work. Now wasn't the time to be stupid. "You're right. I do need to work. I accept your offer. I'll have to get Sammy enrolled in day care before I can start work."

"That's fine. We're working in the gardens right now, readying them to serve as venues. You met Russ Hunter yesterday. Hopefully he can wrap his mind around the idea and design the structure I plan to use for receptions."

Her words confirmed Jane's suspicions that things were not what they seemed between the two of them. "I got the impression he was having difficulties."

Val nodded. "One more thing. I'm keeping everything under wraps at present. So I'd appreciate it if you do the same."

"No problem. In fact, I consider confidentiality part of the job," she said.

Val grinned and said, "I'm going to like

having you around."

It was close to lunchtime when they concluded the interview, and Val insisted she and Sammy join them.

"There's my Sammy girl," Val declared, taking the child from Heath's arms. "Come up to the house."

As Heath and Jane followed along behind, he asked, "How did it go?"

"She offered me a job as her assistant."

"So what do you think?"

Jane swept her hand through her bangs, pushing them out of her face. She needed a haircut. "I don't know, Heath. I've never done anything but manage a coffee shop. That's different from what Val has in mind."

"You don't feel like you can handle the job?"

"I guess I want to believe Val truly needs me," Jane admitted. "She's a good-hearted person who responds to people's needs."

"Oh, I suspect Val knows she'll be the winner in the deal. She's told us how good you were at your job."

His comment surprised Jane. "I should be. I worked there from the time we went off to UK." She'd started out as a clerk and worked her way up. Then the business had sold, and the new owners had no need for a manager.

"Yeah, but there's still work ethics. Not everyone cares about the quality of their work."

"That's true," Jane agreed.

"What does the job entail?"

"Why? You thinking of applying?" she teased at his curious question.

He laughed. "Maybe. I do need a job."

"Val said part of my duties would be helping out in the gardens. Then there's the scheduling for the venues, setting up for weddings, and running errands."

"A Jane of all trades?"

"And master of none," she said with a little frown.

"Don't be so hard on yourself. You think Val knows what she's doing with this new business venture?"

"At least she knows the business from the wedding planning perspective."

Heath shrugged and said, "I remember how nervous she was when she went to work with the wedding planner. She was certain she'd never get through the first day."

Jane felt uncomfortable with his revelation. "I don't think she'd care for you sharing that with me."

"Val would tell you herself if you voiced your concern," he said confidently. "She's not offering the job out of pity, Jane. She needs people she can depend on, and evidently you're at the top of her list."

His words gave her pause. "Thanks, Heath. Truthfully I can't refuse any valid job offer, but you've calmed my fears. I told Val I'd give it a try, and you make me believe I can do this."

"Sure you can," Heath said. "Now let's go see what Opie's prepared to tempt Sammy's appetite."

In the kitchen, Cindy Truelove held Sammy, and the child was all smiles.

"I can't get over how she's responding to all of you. I generally have to peel her off me around strangers."

"Maybe she feels safe," Heath said.

Jane understood how that could be a possibility. She had the same feeling in their presence. Over lunch around the crowded table, Jane sat on one side of Sammy with Heath on the other side. She bowed her head as Jacob Truelove blessed the food and then accepted a serving bowl from Cindy.

"Val tells me she's hired you as her assistant," Jacob Truelove said.

"I've agreed to try the job."

He nodded. "I'm sure you'll do fine. When do you start?"

"As soon as I get Sammy settled in day care."

"Why don't you bring her to work with you?"

Surprised, she looked at Val's mother and then at Val. Thoughts of how little she'd accomplish with her daughter around all day filled her head. "I couldn't," Jane said.

Cindy Truelove's gaze rested on Sammy. "I'd be happy to watch her. I miss having little ones around."

Jane looked at Val again, uncertain what she should say. "I'm sure your schedule is much too busy."

"Not at all. The other children will be out of school soon, and they could help, too."

She would love having Sammy nearby but didn't want to impose on the Trueloves anymore. Jane doubted Val's teenage sister and two younger brothers would appreciate babysitting a two-year-old all summer.

At her mother's hopeful look, Val said, "You might as well bring her along. Mom's not going to be happy until you agree."

A new job and a family of babysitters. Jane didn't know what to expect next. "Well, okay, but if it gets to be too much . . ."

Jacob roared with laughter. "You think one itty-bitty little girl will be too much for a woman who raised seven children of her own?"

"Yeah, Mom will have her doing chores in

no time," Heath said, smiling when his mother tsked at him.

He leaned over and pretended to gobble up the bite of food Sammy held. She giggled and stuffed it in her own mouth. Opie had done well, providing a plate of bite-size foods that Sammy ate eagerly.

"Behave," Cindy told him before she spoke to Jane. "This way you'll be close by when she needs you, and she can see you throughout the day. No separation anxiety."

Sammy had gone to day care almost from birth. Even when he was out of work, Garrett wouldn't care for her, so she spent long hours with other people while Jane worked. She'd only taken her out of day care after she became unemployed and couldn't afford it.

"Jane's schedule will be flexible," Val said. "I'm thinking maybe nine to five thirty or so. Does that sound okay?"

She was used to much longer hours. "I can come earlier if you need me."

Val shook her head. "That's plenty early. Gives you time to drive from Lexington to Paris."

After lunch was finished and the kitchen cleaned, they all went to the horse barn with Sammy to visit the horses.

Evidently Heath had made a major impression, since she returned to him when she wanted something. The sight of Sammy reaching up her tiny hand to him so trustingly made Jane teary eyed.

He swung her up into his arms when Jacob brought out the horse. After his father climbed into the saddle, Heath passed Sammy up to him. Her smile reached from ear to ear when he settled her comfortably and set the horse off into a slow walk. While the Trueloves called out encouragement, Sammy clapped her hands in pure little girl joy and chattered to Jacob.

Heath walked over to stand by Jane's side. "I think we have a budding equestrian on our hands."

Jane nodded. "It's a good thing I took the job. It's Sammy's only hope of coming near a horse."

THREE

Jane found that a routine developed quickly. She arrived around eight thirty, and they discussed plans for the day over a cup of coffee in the Truelove kitchen. Her confidence level increased daily as she mastered her assignments and realized Val hadn't created the position as a kindness to her friend. It felt good to know she could help Val while helping herself.

That afternoon Val went into Lexington and asked Jane to work with Heath in the English garden. She loved being outdoors, so the thought of spending any part of the beautiful day gardening suited her perfectly. The warmth of the sun against her skin made Jane feel like singing as she all but skipped out to the gardens. Heath worked at trimming the hedge wall, and she picked up a couple of handfuls of long clippings and offered an impromptu cheer.

"Come on, let's go! Let's go!" she

shouted, gaining his attention. Smiling broadly, she moved her arms with the snappy motions she'd learned in cheerleading camps. "Trim that hedge! Trim it neat!" She tossed the trimmings into the garbage can with a flourish and added with a clap of her hands, "Truelove gardening can't be beat!"

"Go team!" Heath shouted, pumping the hedge trimmer into the air with one hand. "Jane, you're something else."

"Isn't it a glorious day?"

"I see Val kept you inside too long."

"She said I should work with you."

Heath flashed Jane a welcoming smile. "Where is Val?"

"She went into Lexington to sign papers. I asked why she didn't have them brought out here. She said she can't hide for the rest of her life."

Heath carefully tucked the trimmings from the rosebush into a trash bin. "We've teased her unmercifully about the Val sightings, but she's done a really great job of giving God full credit for the win."

Jane nodded in agreement, rubbing her hands together while she asked, "So what's the plan for today?"

"We can't get more of the material Mrs. Sheridan had laid for the patio in the formal garden, so Val and I agreed it's best to replace the stone. I thought we might get a start on pulling it out."

Jane reached for a pair of gloves. "How much are we removing? Would it work in that little sitting area off the water garden?"

"Hmm." Heath's eyebrows arched. "Great idea. Recycling could save some serious bucks."

"What if we hook up a hose and wash it off as we go?" Jane suggested. "If we had a cart, we could load it, too."

"You're full of good ideas. You hook up the hose, and I'll get the cart."

They worked steadily, prying the reluctant stones from the ground where they had lain for at least three decades. Heath propped and held the stone up while she aimed the hose. She missed, and the pressure of the flow shot dirt and water into the air.

"Hey, watch it," he said, stepping out of the way when her next effort splashed mud on his bare legs.

"Oh, I got you dirty," she said with teasing laughter. "Let me help."

The spray saturated his white sneakers and socks and splattered the cargo shorts he wore.

"Stop it."

"Don't be such a stick-in-the-mud." Jane

laughed when he dropped the piece of stone, splashing even more mud on himself.

"Give me that hose," Heath said, chasing after her.

She aimed protective bursts of water in his direction as she agilely dodged him. Jane turned away when he came closer, and he wrapped his arms around her from behind and wrestled the hose away. After a few seconds, awareness made them both uncomfortable, and they moved apart.

"I'm sorry. I shouldn't have done that."

"No, you shouldn't have," he agreed, rejecting her attempt at remorse by aiming the spray at her legs and laughing when she darted across the yard. Moving target that she was, he still managed to hit her several times with his well-aimed jets.

"Okay, enough," Jane said, brushing her wet hair from her eyes. "We've got work to do."

"Spoilsport," he said with a laugh.

They returned to their task, Heath keeping his distance as he placed the stones against the cart for Jane to rinse. It wasn't long before she felt the results of the strenuous labor in her arms and back.

"Take a breather. You don't have to do it all," Heath said.

"That's what I'm used to," Jane told him.

"Even when I worked all day, Garrett flopped in a chair and stayed there until I had dinner on the table."

"He didn't help with the chores?"

"Wasn't a man's place," Jane said, sarcasm filling her voice as she walked over to a bench and sat down. "His mother told him that. Clarice Holt waited on her husband and son hand and foot. According to Garrett, his parents wanted him to concentrate on football. I was so blind."

Heath paused in loading the stone onto the cart. "What do you mean?"

"I came to Paris from an even smaller town. Guess you could say I started to come into my own about the time I turned thirteen. I filled out, the braces came off, Mom took me to the dermatologist, and I got contacts." Jane couldn't believe she'd told him that. "You should know, very few women are natural beauties."

"I have three sisters. I know how much time you girls spend in the bathroom."

The changed appearance gave her the confidence to try new things. Becoming a cheerleader provided the opportunity to move in a different social group. "Because of Garrett, I became part of the popular crowd. My parents were happy that I was involved in activities at school, but they had no idea what I was doing. To them, I was good little Jane, but peer pressure had me doing things behind their backs."

Heath walked over and sat down next to her. He smiled warmly, touched her hand, and said, "We all do things we aren't proud of, Jane."

Unconvinced, she said, "I made some pretty bad choices in my teen years, but I accepted the outcome. Garrett's life wasn't the only one that changed. I took our vows seriously. I thought maybe we'd become a team. After the baby died, things went downhill from there.

"We went off to UK and got a place in married student housing. He had his football scholarship, and I took a few classes. Then we needed more money, and I took a job at the coffee shop. Then in Garrett's junior year, he hurt his knee, and his football career was over. No more scholarship. I went to work full-time, thinking once he got his degree and a good job that I'd go back and get mine."

Once she opened up, Jane couldn't stop. The words poured out, and she could only wonder what he must think of her.

"It wasn't wonderful, but it was my life. His glory days were over. Garrett started hanging out at the frat house. He never let a day go by that he didn't blame me for ruining his life." She shrugged and said, "I never understood how he came to that conclusion, but maybe I did. At least I played as big a role in ruining our lives as he did."

"I'm sorry, Jane."

His soft apology nearly undid her. No one had ever known what she'd gone through. "It was my choice. I got everything I deserved."

"What happened?"

In an effort to regain her composure, Jane concentrated on brushing the mud from the legs of her jeans. "Garrett flunked a lot of courses and finally dropped out. He took a job selling cars. I think he hoped people would remember him from his football days, but he was never a good salesman. The coffee shop owners saw my potential and promoted me to manager. It wasn't as if we couldn't use the money, but Garrett couldn't deal with my success.

"I nearly gave up on us, but then I got pregnant with Sammy. He seemed happier after she was born. I hoped she'd make a difference for us. But all too soon, he hated her crying and resented her demands on my time.

"I think her real value to him was his

parents' love for their grandchild. He took advantage of them every time he could. He'd say she needed things but never spent their money on Sammy." She pushed up from the bench and took a couple of steps away. "I'm sorry. You don't want to hear this."

"I don't mind listening. You need to talk. Sounds like you're pretty angry at Garrett."

Agonized, she turned back and asked, "How could anyone be so selfish, Heath? He never once thought about Sammy and me or what his action would do to us. If he'd been sick or something, I could understand. But he just gave up on life. Being the 'G man' was all that was ever important to him." Jane remembered the day he'd been dubbed with that stupid nickname. She'd come to detest all it stood for. "Evidently fulfilling that role for your wife and daughter isn't the same as a stadium of adoring fans. I should never have allowed our parents to force us into marriage."

"Then you wouldn't have Sammy now," Heath reminded her.

A sad smile touched Jane's face. "And that would truly be depressing. She's my reason for existing."

"You need more, Jane. What happens when Sammy grows up? You don't want to become one of those women who guilts her child into coming for visits."

"If I'm smart, I'll raise my child like your parents raised you. They will never have to guilt you into anything. You love them too much."

"Love your daughter, and she will love and respect you," Heath said. "But give her wings."

"That's a long way down the road. She's only two."

"Time flies. It's been more than ten years ago that you walked into that classroom. Look at everything that's happened since."

"You've accomplished a lot since then."

Heath shook his head. "I have a couple of pieces of paper with my name on them. You've accomplished more. You're the one making a difference in someone's life."

Jane's mouth dropped open in surprise. She had never looked at her life that way. "I can only hope to be a good mother."

"From what I've seen so far, you're doing a great job with Sammy. She's a blessed little girl."

After Jane left for the day, Heath thought about what she had shared with him. She needed to deal with more than grief. Her anger would destroy her if she didn't forgive

Garrett and move on with her life.

Heath understood internal turmoil. His own feelings of guilt over allowing his family to help him get the expensive education he hadn't really wanted grew stronger by the day. Sure, he'd convinced himself it was for his own good, and he'd worked hard to achieve his goals.

He had put aside his youth and assumed the responsibility of helping his family prepare for the future. Heath loved his twin, but his competitive nature would never allow him to be bested by Rom. That same nature, combined with his father's insistence that no child of his would waste his life, had pushed him to the level of overachiever.

His parents wouldn't have cared what career field he chose so long as he gave it his all. When Rom suggested they get their MBAs, Heath felt that an ability to earn a good salary would enable him to achieve his personal goals even more quickly. An executive job would help him put aside funds for the younger kids' education, allow him to marry and have a family sooner, and not feel he was cheating anyone.

In high school Heath focused on a grade point average that would help him get the scholarships that paid for most of his undergraduate education. Those same grades had helped him get into Harvard.

Up until a few weeks before, their plan had been that he, Rom, and their sister Opie would do their part and use their degrees to help the three younger siblings get their education. There had been no doubt in his mind about what he had to do.

The self-imposed burden that made his high school and college years stressful also made him become an adult at an early age. Failure meant disappointing his family, and he cared too much to allow that to happen. He had no time for fun and games. He'd thought maybe one day he could develop a few of his interests, but there had never been time until now.

Then Val won the money, bought the farm for their parents, funded the younger kids' education, and threw him in a total confusion. For the first time in his life, Heath had no plan for his future.

His nature never allowed him to take things lightly. He'd pushed for years to be able to fulfill his established role for his family. Heath intended to polish his résumé and find the perfect job.

Then he'd come home to Sheridan Farm and the welcome companionship of his family and friends. The peaceful, settled environment always made him feel secure, and now he didn't want to leave. He started helping out in the gardens and enjoyed the work so much that he didn't want to stop.

He hadn't broached the subject with Val. Heath just reported every morning and helped with whatever task she had in mind for the day. He found working in the gardens with his hands comforting. Avoiding the inevitable while enjoying himself as he hadn't done since he was a boy made each day a vacation from his feelings of personal responsibility.

Val had suggested they all consider what they wanted from their futures, and Heath knew he wanted to help Val.

Every time she'd sent him more of her hard-earned dollars, he'd vowed to pay her back. He wanted to work with her on this project. Help her achieve the success she dreamed of having in Your Wedding Place. But he didn't know how to ask her to let him help. He had the feeling she would consider it too much of a sacrifice.

These last few days in the gardens had made him more content than anything he had done in a very long time. Maybe he'd talk with his mother and see what she suggested. Surely he could convince Val that she needed him as much as he needed her. He had a million ideas on how to make the gardens even more spectacular, and as far as he was concerned, all Val needed to do was say yes.

FOUR

May slipped into June, and Jane found herself growing more comfortable with her job and the Truelove family. Val never assigned a task she wouldn't take on herself, and they often worked together. Jane understood Val's frustrations over the holdups with the plans for the new structure and hoped they would soon be resolved.

Heath had so many great ideas for the gardens and impressed Jane with his knowledge of plants and design. She found herself looking forward to the days she worked with him. She did wonder why he wasn't pursuing another job as Rom had done but figured he had his reasons. He certainly was a hard worker, and Jane considered Val fortunate to have his expertise.

It had been a particularly tiring day, and when the phone rang that night, Jane wasn't happy to hear her mother-in-law's voice. At the woman's insistence, she put Sammy on the phone. The toddler lasted a couple of minutes before she dropped the phone and climbed off the sofa. Jane retrieved the cordless and announced her daughter's abandonment.

"Who is this man Samantha's calling *Daddy?*" Clarice Holt demanded. "Who are you seeing?"

"No one," Jane said. "Sammy hears the Truelove children call their father *Daddy* and does the same."

A few moments of silence stretched over the miles before Clarice said, "It's not right."

"She's only two. Mr. Truelove doesn't mind."

"Well, I want it stopped. Garrett is her father. He's the only man she calls *Daddy.*"

Jane found the woman's domineering attitude difficult to take. There had never been any love lost between them. Like her son, Clarice frequently expressed her opinion that Jane had ruined Garrett's life. Jane could do nothing right. Jane had trapped him by getting pregnant. Then after the stillbirth, she'd mocked Jane for being incapable of giving her son children.

Sammy's birth had disproved that, but then she'd been a daughter instead of a son. Then Clarice criticized her skills as a mother. Jane had long since decided that the only way to coexist with her mother-in-law was to ignore her.

"Perhaps you shouldn't take her there. Those places are dirty, and she could get hurt."

Jane nearly laughed at Clarice. A multimillion-dollar farm didn't fit that image at all. "Sammy is well cared for. I don't put my daughter at risk."

"I won't stand for her calling another man *Daddy.*"

"I see nothing wrong with my daughter loving someone who loves her in return." Something fell in the other room, and her child cried out. "I need to go. It's Sammy's bedtime."

Jane knew the conversation wasn't over, and when the phone rang later that night, she wondered if Clarice was calling back to continue her tirade.

"Clarice called me about Sammy calling someone *Daddy.* What's going on, Jane?"

Hello to you, too, Mother, Jane thought. Their long distance interference was a bit much. If they were here, they could see for themselves that the situation was innocent. For that matter, if they were here, Sammy could be spending her days with them. "Clarice is trying to cause trouble. Sammy hears the Truelove kids calling their father *Daddy* and does the same. What's wrong with that?"

"Nothing, I suppose."

"That's what I told Clarice. They're good people, and I'm fortunate to have them helping care for Sammy. She's very happy with Cindy Truelove, and I love seeing her throughout the day. We eat lunch together, and I get to spend time with her when she plays in the gardens."

"Weren't some of their children in your class?"

"Heath and Rom. They were the class co-valedictorians."

"I remember them. Handsome young men. What are they doing now?"

"They graduated from Harvard in May. Rom has a job in Lexington, and Heath is helping his sister with her new business."

"So you're working with the sister and Heath?"

"Her name's Val, Mom."

"Don't be so testy, Jane. I'm just curious about these new people in your life."

"They're very nice. Why don't you and Daddy come for a visit and meet them?"

"Your father is busy at work. And church, of course."

Jane was used to her mother's excuses.

49

Her parents had been too busy to do anything with her since the truth had come out about her and Garrett. After the wedding, they had taken advantage of a job transfer to leave her and Paris, Kentucky, far behind. The loss of her relationship with her parents was one more thing Jane regretted.

"How is my granddaughter?"

"Sammy's doing great. You should see her with the Trueloves. She's not shy at all with them."

"Be careful, Jane. You don't want her upset if this job doesn't work out."

"This job is working just great, Mom. Val assures me she's pleased with my work."

"That's good, but you know your tendency to make unwise decisions."

"One unwise decision," Jane said softly. "Will you ever forget it?"

"I don't mean to hurt you."

"Then why do you do it? I know you and Daddy were disappointed and embarrassed, but I'm your daughter. I made a mistake. Is that sufficient reason to have nothing to do with me?"

"We stood by you."

Jane could almost see her mother's tight-lipped expression. She'd witnessed it enough in those last days before they left. When her parents suggested she give her child up for adoption, Jane asked for time to consider her options. Her mother said there was no time to waste. "No, you married me off to Garrett and left town. Didn't you ever make a mistake, Mom?"

"I'm not having this conversation with you again."

"That's right. Nip it in the bud so you don't feel guilty for not knowing what your wayward child was doing behind your back."

"Good night, Jane. Your father and I are praying for you."

Jane hit the Off button and tossed the cordless phone against the opposite end of the sofa. "Praying." She spat it out like a bad word. She didn't want their prayers. She wanted their love. Why was that so difficult for them to understand?

Thanks to the phone arguments, Jane didn't rest well and then overslept the following morning. When she called Val to explain, her boss told her to take all the time she needed.

Nearly an hour later, Jane set Sammy on her feet in the Truelove kitchen and watched as she ran to Cindy. The woman hurriedly dried her hands and greeted the little girl. Sammy chuckled and held up her tiny arms. Cindy swung her up and squeezed her close.

Sadness washed over Jane as last night's conversation with her mother came to mind. Her parents would never know their granddaughter like this.

"Something wrong?"

She'd noted Cindy's frequent glances in her direction. "Family problems. Garrett's mom started in on me last night, and it went downhill from there. She demanded to know who Sammy is calling *Daddy,* and when I explained that she'd picked it up from your kids, she went off on me."

"Oh honey, I'm sorry," Cindy said, settling Sammy at the table with crayons and paper before coming over to give Jane a hug.

Cindy's gesture of comfort brought tears to her eyes. "I try not to let it bother me, but she says I'm a bad mother."

"Don't you believe it for one second. You're doing a great job raising your daughter."

Jane smiled her thanks. "Sammy is a baby. She doesn't understand the difference."

"Jacob doesn't mind."

She used the tissue Cindy gave her to dry her eyes. "I know. I appreciate the positive male influence in her life. She hasn't had much of a role model."

"You just keep doing what you're doing."

"She says it's my fault Garrett did what

he did," Jane said.

"She's hurting. Lashing out because you've moved on with your life and she can't. Let's not discuss this in front of Sammy. I can ask Jules to watch her if you need to talk."

What was it about these Trueloves? First she'd opened up to Heath about her feelings regarding Garrett, and now she'd done the same with his mother.

Jane stood up straighter and shook her head. "I need to get to work."

Cindy patted Jane's shoulder. "Just remember I love you girls like my own. I'm here for you anytime."

"Thanks," Jane said, somehow managing to get the word past the knot in her throat.

Heath could see Jane wasn't her usual self when she joined him in the garden.

"Everything okay?"

She explained the situation. "I'm so over them trying to run my life but not wanting to help. I'm doing the best I can."

"You're doing a great job. Sammy is happy and healthy. That's what counts. Not whom she calls *Daddy*, though personally I think she's got good taste."

Jane smiled. "She does. Jacob is the best. Now what do you need me to do today? Or at least what's left of the day."

"It's warm today. I thought maybe we'd work on the fountains."

"You want to get wet again?"

Heath shook his head. "I don't plan to put a hose in your hand if that's what you're asking, but I figure we can drain them and clean them up."

Jane eyed the massive fountain in the back of the garden. "Do we disassemble that? It's pretty big."

"We'll start small and work our way up to the big ones. We don't want them looking new. They need to retain that aged look the years have provided."

"So basically we're scrubbing the interior and getting the gunk out of the works so they can keep flowing."

Heath nodded.

"There's a lot to be done now that Kelly Dickerson booked her wedding," Jane said. "I'm so happy for Val. That first booking is a big deal."

"It's definitely a beginning," Heath agreed. "We'll get it done. Do you remember Kelly from school?"

"Vaguely."

"She's nice. Val's not happy about the way she got the referral, but a booking is all that matters."

Jane's head tilted to one side in question.

"Val wanted to keep things quiet," he explained. "She said Kelly knew a lot about her plans, but she and Russ Hunter share an office."

"I never realized just how much there was to starting a business. It seems like a lot of work."

"Start-up can be a challenge. Particularly with something like Val has and going from the ground up. Imagine what it would be like if she didn't have the established gardens."

"Success would definitely be much further away."

"School wasn't easy, but there was a routine about it," Heath said. "I like the newness of this project, but I'm glad I don't have to make the final decisions."

"I know what you mean. I worked at the coffee shop for a long time. I went from waiting tables to being in charge. It's the gradual learning over jumping in feet first. But this is like a new beginning for you all. The future is calling your name, and you can go anywhere you like."

"You, too."

"Not with a child to provide for. When Val first suggested this job, I doubted she needed someone. Boy, was I wrong. It's been exciting and fun. Ordinarily I'd never have considered something like this, but I'm glad I did."

"I've enjoyed being in the gardens again. It's been years since I helped Mrs. Sheridan." He'd spent some of his happiest summers right here in these gardens and feeling particularly pleased when Mrs. Sheridan liked his ideas.

"I'm sure Val appreciates your help, and you do seem to enjoy this type of work. Is it something you'll pursue?"

"Probably only as a hobby," Heath said. "Once I get a job, I won't have much time to work outside."

"Is that why you haven't gone job hunting yet?"

No doubt the rest of the family is wondering the same thing, Heath thought. "I've enjoyed helping Val. I wouldn't mind doing it for a while longer."

"You should talk to her."

Heath didn't know how to make Val understand. She would think he wanted to help out of guilt, and while he felt he should do everything possible to aid in her success, he wanted to do something he enjoyed. At least for a while before he joined the suit-and-briefcase brigade. "Maybe I will."

"What do you want to do?"

Heath wanted to be selfish. He wanted to spend his days sharing the beauty of God's garden with those he loved. But Jane's question was more than curiosity. "It's more about what I'm expected to do. You don't obtain an expensive education and not use it."

"Do you wish you hadn't?"

He shrugged. "I suppose it's like other things in life. Sometimes we want what we can't have."

"I don't understand."

"I'd love to do this full-time, but gardening doesn't pay the bills."

"It could. But aren't you excited? With your degree you can write your own ticket for the future."

The options didn't thrill him, but he'd do what God directed. "I suppose."

"But you've got a college education. It will take you wherever you want to go."

Heath could hear the wistfulness in her words. "You should talk to Val. We've been trying to convince her to go back to college. You should consider doing the same."

Jane shook her head. "I'm sure she's much too busy. As for me, it's not feasible with a small child and a full-time job."

"It's not as impossible as you think. Given this family's philosophy on education, I think there's a good possibility Val would help if you asked."

Horrified, Jane said, "I can't take any more from her. She's all but claiming me as a dependent as it is. She gave me a job. Your mom cares for my child, and I eat at your place more than at home. I'm a definite liability."

Heath could relate. Beyond the work in the gardens, he wasn't contributing anything to the family coffers. "You're not. You pull your weight around here."

And she did. Heath didn't think Val could have found a better assistant.

"Maybe I'll go back one day," Jane said.

"One day what?" Val asked when she walked up on their conversation.

Jane glanced at Heath and back at her employer. "We were talking about the future."

"What about it?"

Poor Jane, Heath thought. There was no way she could avoid this.

"Heath and I were discussing education."

Val glanced at him.

"I suggested she consider going back to UK for her degree."

"They suggested the same thing to me," Val told Jane. "I'm too busy right now."

"It's difficult for me with Sammy and work."

"Would you like to go?"

"Maybe after Sammy starts school."

"You shouldn't put it off," Heath said. "You'll only have more responsibilities then. Like driving Sammy to activities. She'll probably be a cheerleader like her mom."

"I hope not. I'd rather she be like you and concentrate on her education more than her social life."

"A good balance doesn't hurt."

"The wrong focus isn't good. You're all on track with your futures."

Maybe the others, Heath thought. Definitely not him.

"You know where you're headed because you planned and carried that plan through. You'll get there faster."

"So could you," Val said. "We would help care for Sammy if you wanted to enroll in classes. You could probably go a couple of days a week and finish in no time."

"I only had three semesters at UK."

"There's no time like the present," Val said.

Jane looked uncomfortable, and Heath stepped forward. "Speaking of which, we'd better get those supplies if we plan to get anything done today."

FIVE

The days flew past, each so filled with change that Jane had little time to think about anything other than her daughter and work. Now that the venue had been booked, the push was on to get the gardens looking nothing less than spectacular. Since the end of the school year, they had made great progress with the help of the younger True-loves.

When she'd finally thought things might be improving, her landlord sold the house she rented and told her the new owners planned to occupy the residence. Jane knew she didn't want to live in an apartment complex. Moving to Paris seemed the most logical choice. She mentioned it to Val, and the next thing she knew, Val offered her the efficiency apartment above the garage behind the mansion.

Jane wanted to refuse, but then Val pointed out that a number of the farm staff received housing as part of their employment and that she didn't see any reason why Jane shouldn't as well. She argued that having them living closer to the farm would make things easier for everyone. Jane knew it would make things easier for her. Though it wasn't a long drive, she wouldn't mind not having to travel to and from Lexington on a daily basis.

"I think you'd move us into the house with the family if you had room," Jane said when Val continued her efforts to convince her.

She grinned and said, "Well, once Rom finds a place in Lexington, his bunk might be available."

Jane laughed and shook her head. "No thanks. I'll stick with my queen-size bed."

After much thought, Jane accepted the offer. The men moved her and Sammy into the apartment before Heath and Rom left for Boston on Sunday afternoon. Heath had said they needed to tie up loose ends. Jane had no idea what that meant.

The Trueloves quickly absorbed them into their family. She and Sammy ate lunch and dinner at their house on most days. Cindy and Opie insisted there was plenty. Their lively conversation made the meals even more enjoyable.

With Heath gone, Jane worked alone. After Val left to go to Lexington to talk to Madelyn Troyer, Jane carried trays of nursery plants over to the bed Heath had marked on his landscape plan. As she dug in the newly enriched soil, Jane realized she missed him. When she tried to define the role he played in her life, *friend* came to mind. Only a friend would stick around after someone dumped her pathetic past on him.

But there was more. When she looked at Heath, she found it easy to admire the handsome man he had become. When he smiled that sweet, gentle smile of his, she couldn't help but smile back. It was more than his smile. It was his presence. Being with Heath was comfortable. He treated women with respect. She could talk about anything without fear of him belittling her. And when she talked, Jane felt as if he listened and cared about what she said.

While she might consider him as cuddly as one of Sammy's stuffed animals, Jane noticed his muscles when they worked. She'd observed a lot about Heath Truelove and liked what she saw. She couldn't help but wonder why she'd missed it before. Sure, she'd seen the sweet, shy, sensitive Heath, but he hadn't fit into her life then. Was it possible that he could fit now?

Val returned late that afternoon, excited that her former boss had agreed to use the services of Your Wedding Place and would be bringing another potential bride out to look at the gardens. She was even happier that Russ Hunter had created a workable plan and had invited him to dinner that night.

Jane didn't object to being sent home early with orders to join them for dinner and stick around for the unveiling of the plans. Jane arrived to find Jacob angry because one of Val's former coworkers had shown up at the farm cursing, throwing out accusations, and nearly injuring one of the workers with his car. From what Opie told her, the man blamed Val for losing his job.

The incident convinced Jacob and Val of the need to hire security. Jane thought it was a good idea. The security measures would make the farm safer for everyone. She knew she'd rest better.

The evening proved very interesting. Apparently Russ Hunter had redeemed himself with the new plans. Val seated Russ next to her father, and Jane sensed something more in the interaction between the couple. A definite change from that first lunch they shared. When Opie threw out her idea about starting a restaurant in one of the farm outbuildings, there was discussion over whether it was a good idea. That led Cindy to bring up Heath's desire to work with Val on her Your Wedding Place project.

Val's mention of Heath's expensive education made Jane wonder if she would be agreeable to what Heath wanted. She supposed she'd find out when he got back from Boston and they talked. Jane definitely wanted to keep working with Heath. He had such a gentle, peaceful way about him and plenty of good ideas for the gardens.

When the plans came out, a major brainstorming session ensued. Sammy's bedtime came and went. Jane appreciated the way the family took turns entertaining the little girl. After a while Sammy fell asleep in her mother's lap.

"What do you think, Jane?" Val asked.

"It's a perfect addition to Your Wedding Place."

"You believe the structure will interest the brides?"

"Most definitely. Once word gets out that it's here, I'm sure you'll find more than one bride who can't resist the allure of the location."

"Allure, huh? I like that. Remind me to use it in the advertising," Val said.

The resulting laughter caused Sammy to shift restlessly and whine. Jane soothed her as she maneuvered her chair about and stood. "We're going to call it a night."

"You need help getting her home?" Val asked.

"We're fine," Jane said softly.

"I'll walk you home," another family member volunteered.

She smiled her thanks and left the family discussing the plans.

Clarice's early morning call on Monday was the last thing Jane wanted to start her day. "Did you remember what today is?"

She could tell the woman had been crying. Jane had battled a few emotions of her own. Grief mixed with a great deal of anger toward Garrett for what he'd done. "Yes, Clarice. I know."

"Do you plan to take Sammy to put flowers on her father's grave?"

Jane didn't want the child remembering her father that way. "I put an arrangement on his grave for Father's Day."

"Did you take Samantha? Do you ever take her to see his grave?" Clarice demanded, her voice rising to a near screech.

"No, I don't. Sammy has a photo of Garrett in her room, but I don't drag her to the cemetery to pay homage to a grave marker. She's too little to understand what happened."

"No, she isn't. You have to keep his memory alive for her. She has to remember her father."

"What do you want her to remember? That her father was too selfish to be there for her?"

"He was a good man."

She'd heard that one many times over the past year. "Garrett didn't love any of us enough to stick around to fulfill the roles he chose in life, Clarice."

"He didn't choose. You forced him into the role of husband and father."

The sucker punch hit home as the woman intended, but Jane wasn't down for the count. "And he forced me into the role of wife and mother. We both made bad choices. You don't see me taking the easy way out. You seem to think your son would have been better off without me in his life. Well, maybe we both would've been better off if we'd never met. He played as big a part in what happened as I did. I won't accept the blame for his decision."

"You did this to him. Garrett was a good

son." Clarice had obviously worked herself into a fine rage on the anniversary of her son's death.

"He was spoiled and never thought of anyone but himself. Garrett's dead. You'd be better off if you accepted that and moved on. I have no plans to elevate him to sainthood in Sammy's eyes. If she has questions when she's older, I'll answer them."

"If you have your way, she won't know who her father is."

"No doubt you'll fill her in on what a wonderful man Garrett was," Jane said, the words drenched in sarcasm. "You may share the fantasy, but I'll make sure she knows the truth. Sammy is the only wonderful thing that came out of our marriage. Personally, I intend to be around to see my daughter and grandchildren grow up."

Her words hit home, and Clarice responded in kind. "We'll see about that. I have letters Garrett wrote telling what a bad mother you were. I'll take you to court."

"Do what you have to. If you want the real truth about Garrett coming out in a courtroom, we'll go there."

"Don't think you can blackmail me, missy. I will not allow you to destroy my granddaughter's life like you did her father's."

Trembling with rage, Jane shut the phone

off. How dare she make such accusations? Jane had done everything humanly possible to make their marriage work. Garrett hadn't cared about any of them. It wasn't her fault.

Sammy came into the room carrying the horse Heath had given her under her arm and dragging her well-worn blankie. "Mommy cry?"

Jane regretted the angry words as she swung the little girl into her arms and enfolded the child in a hug. More tears came to her eyes as she buried her face in Sammy's baby sweet fragrance. "Yes, sweetness. But Mommy loves her Sammy so much."

" 'Kay. I get down."

The child squirmed for release, and Jane didn't want to let go but knew she had to. Standing Sammy on her feet, Jane managed a smile as she adjusted the hair barrette in the baby fine curls. "Are you taking Horsie to Mrs. Cindy's today?"

Sammy nodded and babbled about her horse. Heath had made a big hit with the stuffed animal he bought in Boston. She hadn't put it down since he'd given it to her the night before. Jane held out her hand. "Let's get you ready to see Mrs. Cindy."

Sammy looked up at her and asked, "Me see Hef?"

Jane smiled. Her daughter enjoyed seeing Heath as much as she did. They had missed him while he'd been away. "Sure. We'll stop by and see Heath, too."

Later they visited in the gardens, Sammy hiding her face in her mother's neck as Heath played peekaboo with her.

"Let me take her to your mom, and I'll be back to help."

They spent the first hour working in silence before Heath asked, "What's wrong?"

Jane supposed her missing nonstop chatter had been a dead giveaway. "Today's the first anniversary of Garrett's death."

His expression of sympathy warmed her heart. "I'm sorry. Do you need to take the day off?"

"Thanks but no. I don't intend to waste another minute of my life trying to understand why he did what he did. His mom called this morning and made a big production over my refusing to take Sammy to visit his grave. She got her jabs in. Blamed me and threatened to use letters he'd written claiming I'm a bad mother to take Sammy from me."

Heath's appalled expression spoke volumes. "That's not going to happen, Jane."

"No, it's not," she said. "It's not the first

time she's threatened me. I don't want to crucify a dead man, but if she forces me to, I will. Garrett may have fooled his parents, but I knew exactly what was going on. He'd call them up and claim Sammy needed something but never spent a dime they sent on her. He'd take their money and buy beer for his buddies. Good old 'G man.' Life was just one big party for him. My parents helped, too. I spent every dime of their money on Sammy. My salary went for the basics — rent, food, and debts. I'm still paying off Garrett's school and credit card loans."

"Didn't he have a scholarship?"

"It wasn't enough. He breezed through every dime he could get his hands on. I tried to tell him there were bills to pay, but he turned a deaf ear. The phone would get cut off, or we'd eat macaroni and cheese or ramen noodles until we got money."

"Why did you live like that?"

"My parents were already embarrassed and disappointed by their wayward daughter. A divorce would have killed them. After Sammy was born, I was determined she would have a roof over her head and food to eat."

"How did they react to what Garrett did?"

"We never discussed it. I suppose it's just

one more major embarrassment in the mess I call my life. My mom is always quick to point out my bad choices. Then Clarice throws her two cents in. I try to be the bigger person and not get into arguments, but they won't let me."

"Mrs. Holt is hurting, Jane."

She understood his defense of the other woman but felt disappointed when he didn't side with her. "So am I, but you don't see me calling her up and attacking her. I try to respect the fact that she's Garrett's mother and Sammy's grandmother, but obviously she doesn't respect me in return."

"Why not?"

Jane shrugged. "I wish I knew. I tried to be a good daughter-in-law. We lived with them after we got married. It wasn't what I wanted, but my parents moved away, and there were no funds to pay for an apartment. Garrett was too busy with football, and I had a difficult pregnancy and couldn't work, but I helped around the house. I went to my doctor appointments alone because Clarice was too angry and my mother was too embarrassed to stand by me. I still remember the day the doctor told me my child had died."

"You were alone?"

Emotion clogged her throat. "I've never

been more alone in my life."

Heath stepped forward and enfolded her in a hug. "I'm sorry, Jane. I wish it could have been different for you."

Tears trickled down her cheeks as she stood there, the memories almost more than she could bear. Garrett insisted they not name the baby after him since he planned on a living son carrying his name. They placed tiny James Edward Holt in a small casket and buried him. His service consisted of her former pastor speaking a few words by the grave site. Her parents hadn't even come for the funeral. Her mother said God always allowed things to happen for the best. The issue of the unwanted baby had been resolved for everyone but Jane. Her lost child would always hold a special place in her heart.

She still wondered why Garrett hadn't asked for a divorce after the baby died. Maybe because he had hopes of them becoming the same carefree pair they had been before the pregnancy. Jane knew they could never be that couple again. Her roles of wife and almost mother for a short time made it impossible for her ever to see things in the same way again. While she grieved the loss of their son, he talked about them going off to college and being free of his parents. He behaved as if their son had never existed, and it broke her heart.

Jane pulled herself together and stepped away. "I'm sorry, Heath."

"You know you weren't truly alone, don't you?"

Puzzled, she looked at him.

"God was there. Waiting, hoping you'd turn to Him in your time of need."

She shook her head. "God wanted no part of me."

"He knew, Jane. Every choice you made, He knew you'd make. That doesn't mean He wouldn't forgive you for making them. All you had to do was ask."

She sniffed and said, "I know. I accepted Jesus as my Savior when I was ten years old." She could see that surprised him. Jane knew her behavior at school showed no indication she loved God.

"What happened?"

She shared the sad story that had become her witness. "When I was older and had the opportunity to make the right choices, I didn't choose Him. I got involved with the wrong crowd, and peer pressure caused me to live a less-than-pleasing life. I'd go and listen to the sermons and know I was sinning, but I didn't stop. We were in church for every service. It got uncomfortable, but

I'd zone out and think about my plans with my friends after church. When I got into trouble, I thought about how I'd sinned and convinced myself I destroyed God's love for me just like I'd done with my parents. After they married me off and moved away, I didn't attend church anymore. Garrett and his parents weren't Christians. Later I worked most Sundays at the coffee shop."

"It starts off by missing one Sunday, and then it becomes easier to miss the next, and before you realize it, you've shifted God out of your life entirely."

"I justified my actions and told myself I wanted to be different, but I wasn't."

"Have you ever thought about going back?"

"I always thought I would. One day."

"Why not now? Sammy needs to attend church with her mother, just like you attended with your parents."

"Let's hope I can be less judgmental if she falls short of my expectations."

"We all fall short, Jane. God doesn't judge us as harshly as we judge ourselves. You should come back to church."

"I'll think about it. I could use a shoulder to lean on, particularly now that I'm responsible for Sammy's future. I want to help her make the right decisions. But it's not really something I can control. She can be president, or she can marry young and be a stay-at-home mom."

"And it doesn't matter as long as she's happy. Don't regret the choices you made, Jane. You learned something from every one of them."

Val joined them. "Are we transplanting the lilies today?"

As Heath and Val discussed the merits of moving the bed, Jane thought about what he had said. She had chosen to love Garrett. Their relationship had changed her plans, but it had been her decision.

What if she'd opted for someone like Heath? Her life would have been very different. For one thing, she'd be educated. The coffee shop had been fun. She liked being around people, but she'd wanted to obtain her business degree and find a job where she could make a difference. She felt like she'd put her dreams on hold permanently after marrying Garrett.

Their discussion stayed on her mind over the rest of the day. Heath's statement about God being there kept coming back to Jane. Knowing He was there watching hadn't kept her from making mistakes. What had seemed thrilling and exciting had taken a turn down a path she didn't want to follow. There was no turning back. No changing the inevitable.

Jane often wondered why she'd been seduced by popularity. Choosing to be one of the in crowd threw her life into a downward spiral until she finally took back control. Learning she was pregnant with Sammy provided Jane strengths she'd never realized existed. She insisted Garrett find work and located a home for them like the one where she'd lived with her parents.

Heath's comfort today reminded her that some men could be kind and loving. If she hadn't fallen for the lies, she could have been with a man who loved and respected her as his wife. A man whose focus went beyond the next sports event.

In her youth, she confused the real gold for the dross. It wasn't too late. She could find a man who would love and treasure her and Sammy. A man who would not feel inconvenienced by their existence. She could have happy ever after.

After lunch Jane returned to weeding and deadheading. The hot days and rain showers provided for a bountiful crop of weeds and grass, and the blooms on some of the flowers didn't seem to last very long. Jules had gone into town with Heath, and the two younger boys were helping their father. Val said she needed to return phone calls, and Jane worked alone.

"So how was the date?" Jane asked when Val came outside. Russ Hunter had invited Val out to celebrate her second booking.

"I enjoy spending time with Russ."

"I'm sure you do. When's the second wedding?"

"The Saturday after Kelly's. Russ suggested we have a launch party. I thought maybe Thursday of that week since we'd already have the tent up. What do you think? Too much?"

Jane let out a low whistle. "That's going to be a challenge, but we might as well get used to turning the areas over quickly."

"I really do appreciate your help, Jane."

They worked companionably for the next hour before they took a water break. They enjoyed the coolness beneath the huge trees as they sipped ice water from the bottles they kept in a nearby cooler. "Okay if we take Sammy to church?"

Right after she moved into the apartment, they had asked if she could go. Jane couldn't think of a reason why her daughter shouldn't attend church with the Trueloves and said yes. Sammy enjoyed her weekly excursions.

77

"I thought I might go, too," Jane said.

"Can I ask what made you reconsider?"

"I've been feeling left behind," Jane said. "Sammy is so happy when she comes home. All of you are reenergized, and I want to experience that for myself."

Val nodded. "We leave around nine fifteen."

"I can drive Sammy and myself."

"If you want but there's room for you both."

"I'll let you know."

On Sunday Jane and Sammy rode in the big SUV with Val, her parents, Opie, and Jules. Heath and the younger boys rode in Heath's truck.

"I should have driven," she said.

"Heath always drives separately," Opie said from behind them. "He says it's good to have a second vehicle in case someone gets sick or there's an emergency."

Jane hadn't thought of that.

They dropped Sammy off in the nursery, and Val, Opie, and Heath took her to the young adult Sunday school class. Jane enjoyed meeting a number of women and men her own age. Offers to join in other church activities and invitations to come back abounded.

"I can see why you enjoy attending church

here," Jane said as they moved to the sanctuary for the morning service. The Trueloves filled the pew but made room for her. "Everyone is so friendly."

"They are wonderful people," Val said. "We leave Sammy in the nursery. She got restless out here. They called us the first couple of weeks, but she stays the entire time now."

Embarrassed, Jane said, "Why didn't you tell me? I should have come with her."

"She's a smart kid. She didn't like sitting on laps and being shushed."

"She's not quiet."

"The structure is good for her, and so is being around other kids her age."

"I probably should get her into more activities."

The music began, and they turned their attention to the worship service. It had been a long time since she'd last attended church, but the familiarity of the experience — the music, the scripture, even the format of the service came to her quickly. The hymns were the same, and she even knew some of the praise songs from hearing them on the radio.

After the service Heath pointed out the various areas of the church when he took Jane to the nursery to pick up Sammy. The child came running, screaming their names.

"We do not yell like that, Samantha Mary," Jane said without hesitation.

Heath swung the child up into his arms, making her giggle before he said, "I didn't know her middle name was Mary. Did you name her after someone?"

"It's my first name." She waited for a comment on the old-fashioned name, but he said nothing.

"I hope she's not too much trouble," Jane said when Heath introduced her to the nursery director and staff.

"Not at all. We love having her with us."

"Mommy. Oah," Sammy called, holding up her picture.

The multihued page was so marked up Jane couldn't make out what it had been. She looked to the other women for an explanation.

The director smiled and said, "It's a rainbow. We studied Noah and the ark today."

She nodded. "I see that now. Good job, Sammy," Jane said with a proud smile. "I'll should find some Bible storybooks. Sammy loves being read to."

"Check our library here," Heath suggested. "They have lots of children's books."

"But I'm not a member."

"No problem. In fact let's go now. You can

choose what you want, and I'll check them out for you. Mom would probably appreciate some extras. They have videos, too."

The variety of books in the library surprised Jane. Sammy pulled books from the shelves until Jane told her to stop. After picking out several she thought Sammy would enjoy, Jane said, "I'm sure everyone's waiting on us."

A few minutes later Heath checked out the books, and they were on their way.

"I've been looking for you," Val called when she spotted them leaving the library.

Heath hefted the pile of books into his arms and said, "Jane wanted Bible stories."

"Good idea." She glanced at Jane and asked, "Did you find anything for yourself? They have some great Christian fiction."

"Maybe next time. I do like to read."

"We have time if you want to look."

Jane wouldn't think of holding them up any longer. "I'll check next time."

"There are plenty of books at the house already," Heath said. "I'm sure you can find something you haven't read."

"I could start with my Bible," Jane said. "I haven't read that in a while."

"Sounds like a plan."

Six

Heath stuck his head around the office door and asked, "Got a minute?"

Val glanced up and said, "Sure, what's on your mind?"

He made himself comfortable in the visitor chair. "I wanted to talk about helping with Your Wedding Place."

Val smiled, stood, and came around to prop against the desk. "I wondered when you were going to ask. Mom dropped that news on me the night Russ showed them the plans."

"What do you think?" he asked eagerly.

"I'm not sure it's in your best interest."

Heath sighed. Opie had already told him about Val's reaction. He understood why she felt as she did, but that didn't ease his disappointment. He'd prayed she'd be receptive to accepting his help. After spending hours planning the direction she could take in the gardens, he wanted to be around to see how they worked.

"But Daddy says we'll both be winners if I agree."

Her words gave him the little bit of hope he needed to continue his quest. He leaned forward in the chair. "I know I need to think about getting a job, but I'm enjoying working in the gardens. Of course I realize I need to add to the family budget, so what if I give back the money you gave me for graduation?"

Val laughed. "Are you trying to pay me to work in the gardens?"

Feeling sheepish, Heath said, "I suppose I am."

Val shook her head. "The money is yours. I've set aside the same amount for Jules, Roc, and Cy. Theirs will be bigger, though, since it's invested, but the initial amount is the same."

"It's not fair to you," Heath said. "Not after the sacrifices you made to help us. You put your life on hold to get the three of us through school."

"Not really. I had to work anyway. I became a better steward of God's money by helping you, and look at how He rewarded me."

"But what about a home and family?"

She shrugged. "God hasn't sent the husband."

"You could have used the money for yourself. Gotten your degree. Improved your life."

"I did it my way, Heath. And I'd do it again."

"I should do like Rom and get a job."

"Rom has future plans. He'll marry Stephanie when she comes home from Africa. He's using his money to help her now and saving for their future."

Heath wanted to feel relieved but didn't. Rom had dated Stephanie throughout college and planned to marry her, but he knew that if things hadn't happened as they had, his twin would have set aside those plans to help provide for the kids' education.

"It's your choice," Val said. "What do you want from the future?"

Heath might be confused about a number of other things, but he was clear on one point. "I'd like to marry the woman of my dreams and have a family."

Val shrugged. "That shouldn't be difficult."

"You'd be surprised," Heath said. Ever since Jane had come back into his life, the idea that they could be a couple lingered in his mind. But his doubts kept him from pursuing her. Her anger at Garrett made him believe she still loved her husband. The fear of fighting a dead man for her affections seemed to be a greater obstacle than he could overcome.

"You can't rush God," Val said. "Let me tell you what I have in mind. You work with me setting up the gardens. I pay you a weekly salary. . . ."

"No way," Heath said. He didn't want to take more of her money. He wanted to pay back a little of what she'd given him.

"I'd pay anyone else I hired, so why not you?"

"I want to help you. You don't have to pay me."

"I pay you, or we don't work together," Val said with conviction. "You need money to cover your expenses."

"I have the graduation money."

"It's invested, and there would be penalties for early withdrawal."

He knew she was right, and while it seemed like a lot of money, it wouldn't take long to spend a big chunk of it on living expenses. "Okay, but you have to let me work."

"Have I held you back thus far?"

"No, I mean more like a job," he said earnestly. "You tell me what you want, and

I get it done."

Val laughed and joked, "It's more you telling me what I want done, but we'll work together to get the job done. Even more now that we've got two weddings and the launch party booked." Val stood and stretched out her hand. "Welcome to the Truelove, Inc. family."

He stood and hugged her. "You're a nut, but I love you."

As he left the office, Heath could hardly wait to share his news with Jane. He found her pulling weeds in the front garden. She grabbed hold of a particularly large specimen and put all her weight behind her effort, only to end up flat on the ground.

He laughed when she waved the offending weed in victory and scrambled to her feet, yelling, "Go, weed!" Heath moved closer and brushed at the dirt on her cheek. "You trying to plant yourself?"

"I could think of worse places to live. Where have you been?"

"Talking to Val. You have a cheer in your repertoire for her agreeing to give me a job helping with the gardens?"

"Yes!" she screamed, doing a little dance before she hugged him. "Congratulations."

Jane's exuberance knocked him back a step, and Heath wrapped his arms around her to keep them standing. When she made no effort to separate, he held her a little longer. "Thanks. I wasn't sure she'd agree at first, but I'm glad she did. I wasn't looking forward to an office job after working out here."

"I can understand that. I've enjoyed communing with nature myself."

"Let me help with those weeds."

"I need muscle. Knock yourself out. I suspect the roots go all the way to China."

The day of Kelly Dickerson's wedding dawned bright and beautiful. Heath had been out since early morning, making certain the last-minute details were finished.

"Happy?" he asked Val when she came out of the house after showing Kelly where her bridal party could dress.

"Oh yes. Kelly is happy, too."

"Then we've done our job," Heath said.

"And done it well. We've come a long way since we started working on these gardens. Mrs. Sheridan would be proud."

After having seen the gardens in their glory, they knew Mrs. Sheridan would have been heartbroken by their deplorable condition. They concluded that Mr. Sheridan's caretakers only performed minimal work after his wife's death. Mowing and weed eating didn't begin to account for the continual grooming and maintenance the vast gardens required.

"I think so. She loved them so much. We should get a sign. What do you think about 'Esther's Garden' for the English garden?"

"Great idea. Let's order little hand-carved signs and tuck them into out-of-the-way places so people just happen upon them."

He nodded. "Any potential brides in this group?"

Val grinned at him. "Maybe one or two."

"Where's Jane?"

"She had an appointment. I told her we'd finish up without her."

Heath wondered what was up but didn't ask.

"You should get dressed if you're going to attend the wedding."

Kelly had invited him, Rom, and Jane to the wedding, assuring them their former classmates would love seeing them. Rom had other plans, but Heath couldn't very well escape when he lived and worked right there at the farm. When Jane said she planned to go, he asked if she'd like to go together. She agreed, and the idea of spending time with her made putting on a suit and tie and frittering away hours with people he hadn't seen in years a little more appealing.

■ ■ ■ ■

"Wow," Heath exclaimed when she walked toward him. "You clean up nice."

Jane grinned. "So do you."

"That's some dress." *And what you do for that dress is fantastic,* he thought. He'd always thought her beautiful, but today she looked stunning. She would turn more than one head.

She held out the little bolero jacket and twirled around on the high heels she wore. "I couldn't very well wear my gardening clothes to Kelly's big event."

Heath offered his arm. "Shall we do Your Wedding Place proud?"

"Why of course."

In the garden entrance, an usher stepped forward and escorted Jane to the bride's side. Heath followed. He noted the way Jane checked out her surroundings. "See anyone you know?"

"Some people from school. One or two I used to see at the coffee shop. Russ Hunter is over there." She indicated his location with a tilt of her head. "I saw him talking to Val earlier. She didn't look happy."

"She's not. There's been a hang-up with the permits." He didn't share that Val

89

suspected Russ of deliberately delaying her project.

Jane leaned closer, and the light scent of her perfume filled his senses. Her voice dropped lower when she said, "I'm so excited for Val. This is a major first for her business. I want to take it all in. Find the areas we can improve on. Maybe even things we could offer that would expand her profit margin."

"Val doesn't expect you to work."

She nudged him playfully. "I know. But I need facts for when we talk weddings tomorrow."

Women and their weddings. He'd never understand the fascination. Men tolerated them for the women they loved, but most of them would rather be stuck in the eye with a hot poker than stand around in a tuxedo for hours on end. "Anything outstanding about this one?"

"Fairly traditional for the most part," Jane said. "But I haven't seen the dress yet."

The attendants came down the aisle in their lavender dresses, lining up to the left of the flowered arch. Most of the greenery was live, and he and Val had added the cut flowers and ribbons earlier that morning.

The bridal march began, and they stood. Jane's gasp when Kelly entered made him lean down and ask, "How's the dress?"

"Fabulous. She's a beautiful bride."

The couple had opted for a traditional religious service with a few extra elements. Afterward Jane and Heath exited the garden with the other guests. She held on to his arm as they walked toward the tent, trying to keep her heels from sinking deep into the thick grass.

"I'm glad we don't have to set up for a reception," he said.

"I'm sure it's just a matter of time before someone asks," she said.

Alex Casey, another one of the high school jocks from their class, made a beeline for them. "Jane, good to see you. You're looking great."

"Thanks, Alex. You remember Heath Truelove."

"Yeah. Good to see you," he said, swinging his hand with one of those cool handshakes Heath detested. "It's been awhile. What are you up to these days?"

"Not much. What's up with you?"

"Took a job in Denver. My girlfriend is one of Kelly's bridesmaids. How's your brother? Can't recall his name."

"Rom is great. He's working in Lexington."

"Excuse me," Jane said. "I need to see

what Opie wants."

The two men watched her walk over to where Opie stood.

Alex released a low whistle. "That's one hot woman. Hey man, can you believe old Garrett killed himself? I always thought he was too egotistical to do something like that. With a wife like Jane, he must have really been nuts. You two dating now? What's she like? Were the rumors true?"

Heath found the man's steady flow of questions offensive. "No, we're not dating. The rumors were all lies. Jane is a decent, loving mother whose focus is on her child. She didn't deserve all that junk that was laid on her then, and she certainly doesn't deserve it now."

Alex's eyes widened. "Hey dude, lighten up. I didn't mean anything."

"Good luck with that job." Heath walked away, confused by his reaction to the man's words. He hadn't expected to feel the need to defend Jane after all these years. Sure, Jane was a beautiful, vibrant woman and men would always wonder if they had a chance with her, but Heath didn't have to like it. Why hadn't he told Alex they were dating? Because in his heart Heath wanted nothing more.

"Everything okay?" he asked when she

returned to his side.

"Sammy couldn't find her horsie. Where's Alex?"

"Far away, I hope." Heath had few dealings with the guy in high school and hoped to have even fewer in the future.

"What happened?"

He might as well tell her. No doubt it would be the gossip of the wedding. "Walk with me."

They went into the garden and sat on a bench, watching as the photographer posed the wedding party.

"Tell me."

"He asked if the rumors about you were true."

She didn't look surprised. "Why?"

"He thought we were dating."

Realization dawned in Jane's eyes. "Alex isn't the first to ask that question. They know me. They know my past. I can't get around that."

Her earlier sparkle disappeared, exchanged for a mask of sadness, and that angered him. Heath served the God of forgiveness. If He could put Jane's past behind her, other people could, too. "It's none of his business."

"Small town, Heath. Everyone makes everything their business."

"It's the past," he insisted. "Alex Casey should leave it there."

"But he won't. They never do. My reputation will follow me the rest of my life. I accept that."

"Why should you have to, Jane? Was what you did so bad that you feel you have to pay for your mistakes forever?"

"Think what you want, but I defend my choices, too. Maybe they weren't good, but I exercised the freedom God gives us all. I loved Garrett, but I never did any of those things people said I did."

"So why didn't you tell them?"

"Garrett said no one would believe me. The guys winked and nudged, and he played up to them. The girls seemed even more determined to fling themselves at him."

"Did he ever . . . ?"

She shook her head slightly. "I don't know. I didn't want to know."

Heath hadn't cared for Garrett Holt. He flaunted his popularity at every opportunity, making everything about him. When Jane chose to date him, Heath worried that she'd fallen victim to that public persona. "Did you let it happen, Jane?"

She shook her head. "No. I had dreams, too. I thought we'd go to college and then have a magnificent wedding. Garrett would work, and I'd be a stay-at-home mom until my kids went to school, and then I'd have my career. Pretty fantasy, huh?"

Heath didn't say anything. Not for him. Heath planned to provide for his family so his wife could be there for their children.

"Learning I was pregnant was a major shock. Everyone had suggestions about what we should do. Garrett suggested abortion, but there was no way I'd do that to my child. Clarice just wanted me to disappear. My parents thought adoption was best. When I wouldn't agree, marriage became the only option. They hustled us off to the magistrate's office and got it done quickly. Our parents made the decisions for us.

"We kept going to school, but things were different. All my friends avoided me. We were living with Garrett's parents, and they weren't very friendly. Mom and Dad moved to Colorado. I didn't have anyone but Garrett and my unborn child."

"Do they know what happened to the baby?"

"The doctor said it happens. Knowing my baby would be stillborn was the worst thing that ever happened to me. I had such high hopes for the future."

"You can't survive without hope," Heath

said. "It's the only thing that motivates us to get out of bed every morning."

"You're right. I still hope to one day prove myself to all these people who saw the bad Jane."

Somehow he had to convince her that she wasn't that person. "Bad Jane is a figment of your imagination," Heath said. He stood and held out his hand. "Come on. They've finished the pictures. Let's get seated before they introduce the wedding party and serve dinner."

SEVEN

Jane watched Sammy pat Jacob's hand to get his attention. It was his birthday, and his family and friends congregated to celebrate. That afternoon he'd injured his leg and been knocked unconscious by a horse. Every family member believed a hospital visit was in order, but Jacob stubbornly insisted on sticking around to enjoy his party.

His smile widened, and he swung the child up onto his lap. Jane smiled when Sammy kissed Jacob's cheek. Sammy wanted to comfort Mr. Jacob's "owie," just as the entire family often did for her.

These were the kind of grandparents her child deserved. Loving, good-hearted people who didn't pass judgment on those they cherished.

"Enjoying yourself?"

Jane glanced at Heath, her heart picking up speed at the sound of his voice. *I'm in trouble,* she realized. Her awareness of him increased with each passing day. Now that her eyes were open to the good qualities a man should possess, she recognized many of them in Heath. Jane particularly loved the way he treated his family.

Earlier in the day, while working with Val to set up the business launch party for Your Wedding Place, her friend had suggested God would send the right person for her and Sammy. As she looked deep into Heath's gaze, she couldn't help but think He already had. That overwhelmed Jane. If only Heath felt the same, but Jane sensed he held back from her and wondered why.

"I'm so thankful your dad is okay. I was afraid when I heard he'd been injured."

"I wish he'd go get checked out," Heath said.

Jane smiled in understanding. "I was here when they brought him in. Val sent me up early to get Sammy. She thought your mom might need to finish a few things." She shook her head. "Cindy was beside herself."

"I'm glad you were here for her."

"Me, too. She does so much for us. Did they figure out what happened?"

"Not really. Evidently Fancy went crazy, and Dad got in the way."

"Why would she act that way? She's the

most docile horse you have."

"We don't know. Bill called the vet to check out Fancy and her baby."

Jane's hand went to her mouth. She hadn't thought about the horse being pregnant. "I pray they're all okay."

"Me, too. Are you ready to eat? Let's check out the food."

Her mouth dropped open. "You can't still be hungry after all that food at the launch party."

"That was snack food. This is meat and potatoes."

Jane laughed and followed him across to the dining room where the Truelove women had set up quite a feast. Opie's gift had been to prepare all of her father's favorite foods. No wonder Jacob objected to leaving his guests and his birthday dinner.

Heath filled a plate, and Jane picked a few things to taste. After taking a bite of the melt-in-your-mouth pot roast, she understood Jacob's objections. "This is wonderful. The tea party refreshments were fantastic, but this is even better."

Heath barely stopped eating long enough to agree. "Food is definitely that girl's calling."

The evening passed quickly, and soon it was

time to say good night. Jane looked down at her daughter sleeping peacefully in Jacob's arms. "Time to take her home."

"You're welcome to leave her here to-night," Cindy said.

"She sleeps better in her own bed. She'll wake the entire house with her cries if we upset her routine."

"I'll carry her to the apartment for you," Heath volunteered.

He scooped up the child and adjusted her against his shoulder. Sammy's eyes flickered open for a moment and then closed. "She's out for the count," he said with a grin.

Jane repeated her birthday wishes to Jacob and told everyone good night before holding the door open for him. "She's not used to so much excitement. You saw how she was in the thick of things."

"Has her mom's personality," Heath commented.

"Let's just hope she makes better decisions than I did."

"Every parent wants that for their child," Heath said. "They want us to make better decisions than they did, and she'll want her children to make better decisions than she does. That's human nature."

Jane wondered if that were true. Her parents had never admitted regretting their decisions, but she wondered if they did.

They moved along the pathway to the apartment, enjoying the beautiful summer night as they walked. Heath followed her up the stairs and stepped aside on the landing while she unlocked the door.

Longing filled her as she wished they were a family returning home for the evening. As she watched him lower Sammy into her toddler bed and kiss her cheek ever so gently, Jane couldn't remove her gaze from him. She could love this man with every bit of her being. In him, she saw everything she needed.

She pulled a light blanket over the sleeping child and turned on the night-light before pulling the door closed behind them. "Would you like something to drink?"

Heath rubbed his stomach and shook his head. "I don't have an empty spot left."

Jane sat on the sofa and pointed at the seat next to her. "I don't think any of you will be hungry again for weeks."

Heath joined her, leaving a space between them. "We'll be ready for the leftovers tomorrow. I hope Dad shares." He leaned back, yawning as he said, "I'm tired. It's been a busy day."

"It's been a busy week. Val's launch party went well. I spoke with a number of interested planners. It's so exciting," Jane enthused. "People asked about booking other events, too. Val deserves this. I'm so happy we've become friends." A thought flashed into her head. "You know, now that I think about it, I didn't really have a girlfriend after Garrett and I got together."

"How did you and Val meet?"

"She used to come into the shop to pick up lattes for Maddy Troyer. She introduced herself, and I asked if she knew you and Rom. We clicked. She's become a good friend. My best friend. She came to Garrett's funeral and brought food to the house. I couldn't believe how supportive she was. She kept coming back."

"That's our Val."

"You're each special in your own way," Jane said, placing her hand on his and squeezing gently. "I'm so thankful to have you back in my life."

They stared into each other's eyes for several moments before she shortened the distance between them and kissed him. Heath looked as surprised as she felt. The kiss left her feeling shell-shocked.

"I'd better go. It's getting late."

She didn't want him to leave. "Stay."

"I'm sorry, Jane. I can't."

Disappointment filled her. "You don't

want to?"

"It's not that," Heath said without hesitation. "But out of respect to you and myself, I can't."

"We're consenting adults."

"Accepting what you offer goes against everything I believe."

"You sound almost like a . . ."

"I am," Heath said before she could finish the sentence. "I'm saving myself for the woman who will become my wife. Purity is a gift. Not to be taken lightly."

"But you're a man," Jane said. "Surely you have . . ."

"I'm normal. I have biological urges, but I control myself. I learned many years ago that life is not about making conquests with women."

"I see," she said, feeling ashamed that she'd thrown herself at him like that.

He took her hand in his and squeezed. "I'm not judging you. I never believed your reputation was as bad as the gossip made it sound."

"Garrett was the only man in my life."

"I thought that was the case."

Their gazes met and held. "Why did you care?"

"I liked you. I didn't want to believe the rumors."

Jane didn't understand. Why would he care what people said about her? She'd heard the rumors, and when she wanted to defend herself, Garrett had said no one would believe the truth. In hindsight, Jane realized the rumors that ruined her reputation enhanced his. "Sometimes I cried," she admitted, her voice so low she wasn't sure Heath could hear her. "I was so hurt that my love for Garrett had been reduced to a bunch of lies."

"Didn't he defend you?"

Heath had defended her. Though she hadn't heard what he'd said, she knew he'd spoken up in her defense. Unlike Garrett, he never worried about their former classmates taking offense. He hadn't worried about what others would think or say. He just spoke his piece and dealt with the consequences.

Jane shrugged. "When I'd get upset or angry, he'd appease me by saying we knew the truth and the others didn't matter. I accepted I couldn't change their minds."

She realized now that the people who mattered respected Heath because he was trustworthy and decent.

"Heath, about this woman you're saving yourself for . . . Do you expect the same purity from her?"

"It's in God's hands. The only thing I can say for sure is that she will be pure in His eyes. Pure in heart."

How could that be? "I don't understand."

"When Jesus forgives us, He washes us clean with His blood."

The reminder of how Jesus had died for her made Jane feel even more unworthy of His love. Her impulsive action didn't reinforce the beliefs she'd been taught to honor. "I'm sorry, Heath. I shouldn't have acted like that."

He looked her in the eye and said, "Sometimes we can't accept the gifts we'd be honored to receive. I can't deny I've always been very attracted to you. You impacted my life that first day you walked into the classroom, but it wasn't meant to be then."

And it still isn't, Jane concluded forlornly. Why had she allowed herself to think she'd ever be good enough for Heath? She was spoiled goods. A sinner in God's eyes. Her life had been in turmoil ever since she'd started making her own decisions.

"I'd better head back," Heath said. "Tomorrow will be another busy day with the prep for Saturday's wedding."

Jane nodded. "Val said Maddy will be here first thing tomorrow to start setting up."

"I'm sure Val is looking forward to seeing

her. She and Maddy worked well together."

She followed him to the door and wished him good night. When he stepped out on the porch, Jane called, "Forgive me?"

He pulled her into a hug, and she went into his arms willingly. "Nothing to forgive. I care for you and Sammy. I always will."

After he left, Jane turned the lamp off and sat in the darkness. When the tears started, she couldn't stop them. Though she understood, his rejection hurt. She'd tried to show him how she felt in the only way she knew how, and he'd rejected her.

Hadn't she done the same to him? In her girl's heart, she'd known the shy smiles and boyish behavior had been more than friendliness. But he wasn't a popular kid. Not even a wealthy one. Just smart, hardworking, cute, and kind. Not someone her immature self would have considered a soul mate.

That had been then. Now Jane knew she'd feel honored to be Heath Truelove's woman.

"Help me, God," she whispered into the darkness. "I've made so many mistakes in the past. Change my future. Direct my path. Make me a good enough person to be Heath's friend."

Heath paused when the lamp went off in

the apartment. He loved Jane. He always had, and walking away from her just now had truly been among the most difficult decisions he'd ever made. He had no other option. He could unite himself with Jane, but without God's presence in their lives, nothing would ever be right.

"Help her, Lord," he prayed. "She needs Your magnanimous love more than she realizes. Only You can reassure her fears and doubts and help her see she's always been loved by You."

He turned and walked toward the house.

"Everything okay?" his father asked when he came into the sitting room.

"Not really." Heath dropped down on the sofa next to his mother. It was getting late, and the others had already gone to their rooms.

"Want to talk about it?"

"I'm in love with Jane. I think I've loved her since the first moment I saw her."

His dad nodded. "I can see how you feel."

Heath started. He hadn't thought he wore his heart on his sleeve.

"It's not that obvious," Jacob reassured him.

"She's grieving still. I admire Jane. She's accepted full responsibility for the choices she made when she could easily blame Garrett."

"Jane is a good person," Cindy said. "But is she a Christian?"

"She believes," Heath said. "Jane attended church with her parents as a young girl. She told me she accepted Jesus as a child. It was only after she became a teen that she fell away from Him. She thinks all is lost because she fell in with the wrong crowd and made wrong decisions."

"Life is about choices, Heath. We can't help but reflect on how different life is when we choose the right path or even when your heart pulls you along the wrong path. I know you want a wife and family, but don't let your desire to find the right woman push you to make a wrong decision."

Heath shrugged and said, "I think I've found her, but I can't be sure. I wasn't the man she wanted when we were in our teens. What if that's still the case?"

"God can change anyone, son. This family is living proof of that."

"We are. My commitment to God is not something I take lightly. He's always first in my life. Even when I'd like to follow my heart."

"Never allow your heart to rule your head," Jacob cautioned.

■ ■ ■ ■

Jane went to bed, but when sleep wouldn't come, she felt the need to do something. Packing boxes from their house sat in the corner of her bedroom. After his death, she'd donated Garrett's clothing with the exception of his letter jacket and football jersey. She'd saved those and some of the trophies for Sammy. She had put off sorting through his personal effects and papers for over a year now. She'd used her work schedule and time spent with the Trueloves as excuses, but truthfully she didn't want to mess with the stuff. Jane didn't want to be alone with her memories of Garrett.

The realization that she'd probably have more alone time now that she'd all but attacked Heath hit her hard. His family would be disappointed when they heard what she'd done.

She should have known better. Blame it on the night. A wonderful evening, filled with good friends, people who didn't hesitate to show their love. When she'd witnessed his tenderness with Sammy, it had been all she could do not to throw her arms around him and never let go.

Was Val right? Would God send someone

to love them? Maybe she should give Him a chance to provide. She hadn't done well on her own.

Even though they had been infrequent, she missed the good times with Garrett. They had enjoyed each other's company, and in his own way, Jane believed he had loved her. He just loved himself more.

She sat down on the floor and dug into the first box. If she was going to dwell on the past, this was the job for it, she thought as she lifted out a number of pictures. She studied the framed shots of Garrett in his uniform, reminded of a time when they had decorated their first apartment. Most newly-wed couples had beautiful wedding photos but not them. They had Garrett's glory shots with a couple of small photos of them as a couple. Thinking Sammy might enjoy them one day, Jane slipped them from their frames with the intention of placing them in a scrapbook for their daughter.

She emptied the box quickly and put the frames back inside. Dragging over another box, she found his personal papers. A small bankbook inside a brown envelope gave her pause. She opened it to find that Garrett had started a savings account for Sammy on the day she was born. Though there wasn't a lot of money in the account and at times the withdrawals had exceeded the deposits, it pleased her to know he had cared about their daughter's future.

Oh Garrett, why didn't we ever really talk? So much of their lives had focused on Garrett and his needs and her anger because he wasn't the man she expected him to be. She laid the passbook on the nightstand.

As she continued to dig, Jane found herself pulled deep into memories of the past. She removed tax files from the records and laid aside old check stubs and medical bills for the shredder. One bill caught her eye, and she picked it up. Why had Garrett visited an oncologist? What else hadn't he told her?

The long day began to catch up with her, and Jane yawned widely. Rubbing her face wearily, she laid the paper on the nightstand with the passbook. She'd call the office and ask some questions. Probably a follow-up for something that he'd considered too insignificant to mention.

She returned the boxes to their corner and turned out the light. The tears came many times in the cover of darkness. Jane went back to another time when her insecurities had held her hostage. Garrett cajoled and threatened, and the anxiety over his true feelings for her never left Jane. Did he love her, or had her refusal to give him what he wanted become a personal challenge for him? He certainly had told her often enough that there were other girls who didn't have her hang-ups.

Those insecurities had precipitated the action that made her a woman before her time. She had cried that night, too. The overwhelming feeling behind her error in judgment had eaten at her. She'd tried to justify it, but knowing how much her action displeased God made it even worse. The purity she'd been taught to cherish had been lost. She couldn't undo what happened, and mistake or not, her only option was to go forward with life.

Based on her experience, she'd advise any young woman to wait. She had considered herself old enough to make her own decisions, and because of that, she'd been forced to deem herself mature enough to live with the outcome of those decisions.

She learned the hard way that planning to wait meant keeping yourself from temptation. No one should pressure others into making choices.

Jacob and Cindy Truelove had been able to impart this knowledge to their children. Val told her the rule was they couldn't date until they were sixteen. The rule was the same for boys and girls. Even then they were told to choose carefully.

Their parents had to be introduced to every person they were involved with, and people who couldn't deal with family couldn't be involved with the Trueloves.

She'd asked how that affected them about dating someone their parents didn't approve of, and Val had said it was a nonissue out of respect to them.

Today's kids might look down on that arrangement, but given the mistakes she'd made, Jane could see the merit. She cuddled under the blanket, watching night transition into dawn. Only time would indicate whether she'd made a mistake with Heath last night.

Jane woke with puffy eyes, and no amount of makeup disguised the fact that she had cried into the night.

Sammy wandered around the bedroom while Jane dressed, finding her way into the keepsake box Jane had set off to the side. The child pulled out her pom-poms and cried when Jane took them away. One look at her sad face made Jane give in.

At the Trueloves', the women and Heath cheered with Sammy as she dragged the pom-poms around the kitchen.

"Why so glum?" Val asked when she set

the cup of coffee before Jane.

She smiled her thanks and took a sip before she said, "I know it's silly for a grown woman to hold on to mementos like that, but I didn't want her to have them," Jane said.

"That's not silly. We'll tell Mom and Opie to hide them when Sammy gets sidetracked. You can pick up a little girl set in Paris."

"Thanks, Val." She finished the coffee and took her cup over to the sink. After rinsing and placing it in the dishwasher, she kissed Sammy and headed out to work. Heath followed.

She glanced at him. "I suppose you think I'm being silly about the pom-poms."

"No. We all have our keepsakes."

She stopped walking and turned to face him. "Maybe I should let them go. Cut myself free of the past."

"Not until you're ready. I'm sorry about last night," he said.

Jane felt deep shame and looked away. "I apologize for making you feel uncomfortable."

Heath caught her chin and pulled her face up to look into her eyes. "Don't. It wasn't my intention to hurt you, Jane. I just need you to know what's important to me."

"You have to find the woman who shares

your beliefs."

He nodded. "Yes, she has to believe."

She believed in God. Her relationship wasn't much to speak of, but she did believe Jesus Christ was God's Son and died for her sins.

Heath cleared his throat and said, "I hope you don't take this the wrong way, but I care about you, and I don't want to hurt you or see you hurt by someone else. You are grieving your loss and reaching out to others for comfort. Not all men are going to say no."

Before she could speak, he raised his hand. "Let me finish. Think before you take that step. Make sure the man you choose can be everything you need. I'd say the same to my sisters."

"I'm not your sister."

Jane wanted to be insulted that Heath would think that of her, but what else could he think? She'd thrown herself at him. He couldn't know she wasn't looking for other men. Only him.

Heath watched her leave. Things would be so much simpler if she were his sister. When he offered his advice, they knew it was out of love. He wouldn't have to deal with the mixed-up crazy emotions that had him running outside to corner Jane early this morning. Or fear he might have done more harm than good with his comments. He loved her, but until he had his answers from God, he couldn't show that love as anything more than a friend.

"Oh, Heath, there you are."

He turned as Val walked around the corner of the house.

"What's up?"

"I need someone to run into Lexington and pick up the chair covers Maddy rented. She's nearly here and realized she forgot them."

"Sure. Do you want me or Jane to go?"

She considered his question for a moment and said, "Jane. We'll need your help unloading Maddy's van."

"I'll find her."

"That's okay," Val said, pulling her cell phone from her pocket. "I can call."

Probably best, he thought. No doubt he was the last person Jane wanted to see right now.

"I took the displays down in the tent," he said. They had moved out the food and serving trays but left the other stuff with the intention of returning later. Their father's injury had thrown everything off kilter, and they had hung around the party until it was

116

too late to get it done. "Where do you want to store them?"

She held up a finger while she gave Jane her instructions. Pushing the phone into her jeans pocket, she said, "Somewhere they'll stay dry. I hope to use them at other events. Maybe I can get Maddy to put one of the smaller signs in her office."

"I'll put them in the office until you decide."

"Thanks, Heath."

They spent a hectic day helping Maddy, but by the end everyone was satisfied with what they had accomplished.

"I'm so thankful I could set up today," Maddy said. "There's no way I'd get all this done if I had to wait until tomorrow."

"Looks like the bride's got a lot of stuff," Heath said as they removed another load from the van.

"There's more on the way," Maddy said. "I'm not even sure they'll be able to see the garden for everything she wants to add."

He stopped unloading and asked, "She's not thinking of altering the garden, is she?"

"No. The garden is fine. She wants to hang lanterns in the tent and has these elaborate table arrangements. There's special china, stemware, and silverware. She even wants the table and chairs changed out. I told her the chairs would be under the covers, but she insisted." Maddy shrugged. "It's her money. As long as she can pay the tab, we'll give her whatever she wants. I hope the rental truck gets here soon. I need to make sure all that stuff is on-site."

"I'll let you know as soon as it arrives."

Jane returned with a truckload of boxes.

"Are all those chair covers?"

"I don't know. They kept loading boxes into the truck. I didn't know what to expect."

Heath turned and called to Maddy. "Where do you want all this?"

"Along the walls of the tent for now."

"From all Maddy says, I think we might be in for a wild ride with this one," he said to Jane.

"I'm sure every wedding will be different. At least Kelly was pleasant to work with."

Heath wheeled a cart into place and began shifting boxes. He looked up at Jane on the back of the truck as she pushed the boxes toward the tailgate. "Still upset with me?"

"Let's not talk about it anymore. I made a mistake last night."

He caught her hand. "You didn't understand."

"Well, I do now. You can relax. I won't be

throwing myself at any other men. I let myself get caught up in the celebration last night and had a lot of mixed emotions when you walked me home."

"I have mixed emotions, too, Jane. Lots of them."

She stared at him for a moment. "Just don't hold my misguided act against me. I'll get myself sorted out eventually."

"Friends?"

She nodded in agreement and offered her hand to shake on it.

EIGHT

"So what's the plan for today?" Jane asked Heath when she saw him crossing the yard. She'd attended church with them on Sunday, and he'd treated her as usual. None of the family had commented on her wayward behavior, so just maybe it wasn't going to be as bad as she feared.

"I'm taking the day off. Want to come along?"

She didn't know what to think. Spending the day with Heath appealed to her even though she knew it was senseless. "I'm sure Val has all sorts of things that need doing."

"You've worked two weekends in a row. You're due a day off. Ask Val. She'll tell you."

"Sammy . . ."

"Baking cookies with Mom. Last I saw, she looked like a ghost under all the flour."

A wry smile touched Jane's face. "I can't compete with cookies. What's the plan?"

"I want to visit Wallis House and the Bernheim Arboretum and have lunch in Paris."

After their discussion, Jane went off to clear her schedule and make sure Cindy Truelove didn't mind babysitting Sammy. A half hour later she waited by the truck for Heath.

"Sorry about that," he said when he finally appeared, pulling the keys from the pocket of his cargo shorts. "Dad asked me to give him a hand getting into the living room."

"How's he doing today?"

"His leg's swollen, and his head hurts."

Jacob Truelove had seen the doctor on Friday and learned he had a concussion and a severe contusion. He'd joked about all the C words the doctor used.

"He's chafing at the bit to get out and do things."

"Maybe I should stay here. Your mom needs to take care of him."

Heath shrugged. "He won't let her coddle him. I figure Dad will read Sammy her favorite book, or they'll watch her favorite movie, and he'll feel like he's helping Mom instead of being useless."

Jane hesitated.

"You'll help Mom more by going than by staying."

He opened the passenger door and stepped aside for her to climb in.

"The forecast says rain today. I hope they're wrong."

Heath laughed and said, "It wouldn't dare rain on my day off."

Jane laid a brown envelope on the seat. "Val asked if we could take these papers by the courthouse. She said Mr. Henderson should be there."

"I don't see why not."

"You were right. Val said I should take a couple of days off."

"I knew she would. Although I'm not sure my plans are what you had in mind."

"Tell me about this place."

"Wallis House is the 1851 home that serves as headquarters for the Garden Club of Kentucky and has an arboretum with lots of native and flowering trees and plants."

"This sounds work related."

Heath shrugged. "You never know where you'll find ideas."

"You need to learn how to have fun," Jane said.

He talked about what they would see, and before she realized it, he had parked in the courthouse square. "You should come inside and take a look. I did a paper on

Paris's historical sites, and this was one of them."

They walked up the high steps and into the building, their footsteps resounding on the marble floors as they walked toward the courtroom in their search for Val's attorney.

"Very *To Kill a Mockingbird*-ish," Jane said in a low voice as she studied the old wooden chairs and balcony area.

"I think they filmed a remake or something here," Heath said once they were back in the hall.

"All this marble must have cost a fortune."

"This is the fourth courthouse. The others burned. They just finished a million dollar renovation to preserve the building. Let's go up so you can get a better look at the paintings."

They walked up the stairs and over to the rotunda to view the artwork illustrating the four seasons of farming in Kentucky. "What's that?" Jane asked, pointing to one of the scenes.

"Hemp. Back when it was used for rope instead of the more well-known illegal use today."

Jane turned slowly, looking at the paintings and then the interior of the building. "Incredible."

"A friend says today's buildings aren't

meant to be around in a hundred years," Heath said.

"Definitely not the same quality construction," Jane said.

"Ready for Wallis House? It's another example of a fine house with staying power."

"It's looking gloomy out here," Jane said when they exited the building. They were almost to the truck when the rain started. She took off running and jumped inside the vehicle, shivering when the rivulet ran down her back as she brushed the water from her hair. She said, "Guess the weatherman knew what he was talking about."

"You want to go home?" Heath sounded disappointed.

"No. I won't melt. You have alternate plans?"

"We could visit Hopewell Museum. I researched it when I did my paper."

"Lead the way."

The rain didn't let up as Heath drove over to the museum and parked. They made a dash for the building, and Heath held the door for her, impressing Jane with his gentlemanly behavior. He performed the tasks automatically but managed to make her feel very special. He guided her to the left and said, "It was the old post office. See that window?" Her gaze followed his pointing finger. She nodded.

"That's where the auditors viewed the workers. They would climb ladders from outside to sit up there and watch. Later they installed a spiral staircase. It's in a closet at the back of the building. The workers didn't know when they were in the building."

Jane followed Heath through the area, finding him both interesting and entertaining as they discussed the various displays. "You know a lot about the museum."

"I spent a lot of time here." He pointed to the floor. "They have marble, too. Just in the public sections of the building. The workers got wood floors."

They wandered through the rooms and enjoyed the artists' paintings on display.

"There's the gift shop, and this is the computer room," Heath said. "Too bad they didn't have this when I used to come here. The old safe is in those closets," he said, pointing to the back of the room.

"I'm impressed. You could be a tour guide for Paris."

"I love history. We'll have to come back for Wallis House, Duncan Tavern, and Claiborne Farm another time. Ready for lunch?" He glanced out the window. "I think the rain has slacked off." On the way out, Heath tucked a donation in the box. "I thought we might eat at the emporium and look at antiques after lunch."

The ambience of the place made it a good choice. Dr. Varden had built the drugstore in 1891. The interior of the store was lined with South African mahogany and Tiffany & Co. stained glass. Over their lunch of chicken salad and fresh lemonade, the conversation turned to the future.

"I want so much for Sammy," Jane admitted. "I hope she doesn't follow in my footsteps. Your family is a good role model for her."

"You're a better role model, Jane. Why are you so down on yourself?"

"I lived two lives, Heath. At home I was good little Jane. Model student, cheerleader, polite, well behaved, and in church with my parents. But at school I became popular Jane. Some areas overlapped, but that life was about Garrett. I loved him. You know what I don't get," she said with a wave of her hand. "Why didn't you get caught up in the peer pressure?"

Heath shrugged. "I suppose my sole focus on getting good grades kept me too busy to care about popularity."

"Too bad I didn't have that problem," Jane said with a self-deprecating laugh.

"You said you turned into a swan," Heath

offered. "Maybe you were flattered by Garrett's attention."

Jane felt her skin turn warm. "Not a swan. But you're right. I did enjoy the attention. Of course that changed fast. Ever since they found out, my parents have questioned every choice I've made. They actually suggested I have my baby and put it up for adoption. Their grandchild! Would your parents do that?"

Heath didn't need to answer. She knew they wouldn't. Jacob and Cindy would welcome the child into their home. They would care for their grandchildren. Not label them as mistakes. Jane laughed and said, "My dad said a jock couldn't support a family, but they forced me to marry Garrett. The entire ordeal was very stressful." She sighed and said, "See what you get? Make one simple comment, and I turn it into my life story."

"I don't mind."

"I know you don't. You're a good man, Heath Truelove. The best. I promise to be a better friend than I was in high school."

"The past is behind us, Jane."

"Is it really? I don't think the past ever truly lets go."

"God forgives us. Our sins can be as far away as the east is from the west."

"I suppose I can't forgive myself. Knowing how much God loves me and how I let Him down is a load to bear. I appreciate the fact that you and your family are Christians. You're good people. That's why I agreed to let Sammy go to church with you. But I'm not sure there's a place for me there anymore."

"Jesus didn't insist you carry your own cross," Heath told her. "He carried it for you."

"I know. I'm praying about it. For now, it's really important to me that Sammy's in church."

"God's house has a place for everyone. Sammy likes church. She enjoys her class and the other kids."

Jane nodded in agreement. "I love your mom, and I know Sammy loves her, but I wonder about that connection with other children."

"Maybe you should find other activities for her. What about ballet? She'd be a cutie in a tutu. I see her dancing around to Mom's radio at the house."

The idea had merit. "Or gymnastics. I suppose I could afford classes since Val has been so generous."

"I wouldn't mind helping out."

"No. I have to draw the line somewhere.

You and your family are far too generous."

"We've been blessed," Heath said. "And Dad says we need to pass that blessing on."

"To the less fortunate?" Jane asked.

"I wouldn't even suggest that. I think Sammy's very blessed to have a mom like you."

After lunch Heath picked up the tab, and they checked out the gift shop before they headed for the truck.

"Do we have time to run by the super-store to pick up something for Sammy?"

"She's already got tons of toys," Heath said.

"I wanted a set of pom-poms for her. I suppose I could drive back tonight."

Heath shook his head. "We'll go. What else are you going to get?"

"I have to see what speaks to me."

"You mean something that talks?" he asked, confused by her words.

Jane laughed. "No, silly. You have to think like a two-year-old. See what toy you think she'd love the most."

Heath shook his head. "The only certainty is nothing you buy is going to entertain her longer than two or three minutes."

"Yeah, but your mom has her putting one thing back before she takes out another. That's a gigantic step forward."

He laughed. "You learn to do that with so many kids, or the house would be unlivable. Of course, Sammy tries to pull one over on the rest of us. She dumps everything out, and when we tell her to pick it up, she says, 'You do it.' "

"Sounds like my Sammy. She cried when I made her help."

They spent the next hour examining every toy in the aisles.

"It's like the three bears," Heath said. "Too old, too young, and just right. What about this?" he asked, holding up a huge boxing glove.

Jane looked appalled. "Not unless you want her beating up on you."

"We didn't have lots of toys," Heath said as they walked through the aisles. "Mostly we played outside."

The need to show him how to have fun overwhelmed Jane. "You have to pick something out, too. I'm buying you a present."

Heath frowned and shook his head. "Don't waste your money."

Jane refused to listen. "I know exactly the thing." She dragged him over to the remote control cars. "We'll buy two and race."

Heath looked embarrassed.

"Come on," she said. "It's fun." She hit a button, and raucous carnival music played while a voice spoke.

"We'll buy them for Roc and Cy."

"They can play with them, but I'm buying them for us," Jane insisted.

"Okay. Okay," Heath agreed. "It's your money."

"You'll play with me, won't you?"

"Sure. Looks like fun."

Jane punched him in the side with her elbow. "You know you wanted to all along. You work hard. You need to learn how to play. Which one should I get?" she asked, juggling the cars as she pointed to two of the books.

"You could put the cars back and buy both."

She grinned and reached for a book. "Or I can buy her this one."

"And I'll buy the other one," Heath said, taking it from the shelf. "We'll keep it at the house."

"Where are we going to hold our race?"

"Depends on what kind of terrain that little car you bought can handle. Flat open, we can use the pathways to the barn. Or more rugged, we can head for the hills."

"Oh, I think my car can beat yours on the hills," Jane returned confidently. "I'll even give you a learning curve."

"I'll take it."

Later that afternoon the rain moved on and the sun shone brightly when they met for their race. When Cy and Roc got word of the competition, they told the others, and soon Val, Opie, Jules, Sammy, and their mom gathered to see what was going on.

"You should have seen his face when I said I was buying him a toy," Jane told the women. "Heath needs to learn to be a kid again."

Val took her mother's handkerchief and said she'd be the starter. When she gave the go-ahead, Jane's car shot forward. The group meandered along behind them as they raced their cars along the pathway. Jane's laughter was a constant as she managed to obtain the lead while Heath's car raced every way but straight ahead.

"I don't know what to do with this thing," he grumbled.

Jane stopped long enough to show him a few of the basics and then frowned when he managed to get his car several yards ahead of hers. "No fair."

"Learning curve, remember?"

"You just look out, Mr. Truelove. I can be

132

a speed demon when the situation warrants."

NINE

"Is the move still on for tomorrow?" Heath asked Val as they walked back to the house.

"Opie and I have been moving boxes a few at a time. We need to pick up the pace. Summer is winding down, and the kids return to school soon."

When the family came to the agreement to move into the Sheridan mansion, Heath found himself torn over living in such a fine home. Granted, their lives hadn't been the same since Val's win and he wouldn't mind having a larger bedroom, but he missed having Rom around during the week. His brother was living in Russ Hunter's spare room and coming home on weekends. Some nights he showed up for dinner, but it was different.

As twins they had been inseparable for twenty-four years. They shared the same room with their younger brothers. They drove back and forth to UK together, and

Uncle Zeb had offered them a finished room over his garage when they lived in Boston.

They hadn't experienced a traditional college lifestyle, but they had been together. In a way, Heath figured this separation was good preparation for the future when Rom married Stephanie and they became permanently separated. He missed his twin and wondered if Rom felt the same way. "Want me to help with the move or work in the garden?"

"The next bride requested the English garden. Other than a few requested changes, it's ready, so let's get moved and settled. Once that's out of the way, we can get back to work on the business."

Early the following morning they loaded boxes into the truck and drove over to the mansion. Cindy had taken the younger kids into town for school supplies and doctor appointments. She'd offered to take Sammy, but Jane knew the little girl would tire too soon and give them a hard time.

She settled Sammy in the office with her books and toys but had her doubts about her daughter's staying power. Jane carried her box upstairs and checked in on the trip down. Sammy had abandoned the items in favor of a video someone had turned on for her.

"Why don't you take her home until Mom gets back?" Val asked when she walked up on Jane peeking into the office.

"Let's give this a try. If she refuses to listen, I'll take her."

Jane and Val got into a routine, taking the boxes from where Heath stacked them to the various rooms. They had just placed their last boxes in the bedroom when they heard Heath cry out Sammy's name.

The crashing sound along with some other indistinguishable cries had them running to find Sammy, Heath, and the box lying at the foot of the curved staircase.

"What happened?" Jane knelt by Sammy's side. Her daughter's pained cries were interspersed with two words: "Mommy. Hurt."

Heath tried to shift his leg, and Jane saw him writhe with discomfort. "I had that tall box and didn't see her. Is she okay?"

She tried to check her daughter for injuries, but the child cried harder when she touched her right forearm. "I think her arm might be broken."

"Oh, Sammy baby, I'm sorry," he said, anguished over what had happened.

"It's not your fault," Jane said. "I should

have taken her home. What about you?"

"My leg."

"I called 911," Val said, tossing Jane a throw as she knelt by Heath's side and spread the second blanket over him. "How bad is it?"

He sucked in a deep breath and said, "Bad."

"What happened?" Opie demanded when she came into the house. "Daddy said there had been an accident."

"I tripped over Sammy on the stairs, and we fell. I tried to grab her, but I was afraid the box would hit her. She could have been killed." Heath shuddered at the thought.

"I left her in the office with her toys," Jane said. "I thought she'd play for a while."

"I know," Heath said. "Last time I looked, she was watching the video. I should have checked again before climbing the stairs."

The paramedics arrived and splinted Sammy's arm and Heath's leg.

"Take her and Jane in the ambulance," Heath told them. "I'll go in the truck."

Jane climbed inside the vehicle and tried to comfort her child while Val summoned their driver to help Heath out to the vehicle. Opie promised to come as soon as she finished her job at Wendell Hunter's.

■ ■ ■ ■

Everyone but Heath returned home much later. Sammy had fallen asleep, and Jane waited while Val unlocked the apartment door.

"I'm so sorry Heath got hurt."

"Jane, stop," Val ordered. "It couldn't be helped."

"I could have taken her home."

"I could have insisted," Val agreed. "But it never occurred to me that this would happen. The most important thing now is to get through it. Why don't you put her to bed? I'll bring you something to eat."

"I can fix something later."

"I'm sure there's food at the house. It will only take a few minutes."

Jane agreed, not certain she could stomach anything right now. After Val left, she dialed Heath's hospital room. Steve, the physician's assistant, had convinced Heath to stay. He sounded very fuzzy when he answered the phone.

"It's Jane. I just wanted to see if you're okay. Do you need anything?"

He murmured something that sounded very much like "love me." She must be losing her hearing. "I'll let you sleep. And say a prayer for your healing."

After another mumbled response, Jane hung up the phone.

Oh, why hadn't she taken Sammy home? Didn't she have enough to make her look bad to Heath already? As her mother would say, another bad choice that hurt someone else. One she'd have to live with for weeks.

Val returned with food and instructions for her to take a few days off to be with Sammy. "But you have to get moved, and there's that wedding next weekend."

"I can hire a mover or even get some of the guys to help out. Don't worry. We'll get it finished."

"I want to do my job."

Val shook her head and said, "You're officially on sick leave until Sammy is feeling better. Don't argue with your boss."

Later Jane did what she'd put off for hours. Drawing a deep breath, she prepared for censure as she called Sammy's grandparents to tell them about the incident. Her parents weren't home, so she left a message for them to return her call. Clarice answered the phone on the first ring.

"He could have killed Sammy."

Clarice's reaction to the incident didn't surprise Jane, and she defended Heath. "It was an accident."

"Why are you standing up for that man? He broke your daughter's arm."

"Because it's not his fault." If anyone was to blame, it was she. If she'd made the right decision, the incident would never have happened. Heath wouldn't be in the hospital, and Sammy wouldn't have a cast on her arm. "Sammy had no business on the stairs."

"What happened to that woman who keeps her while you work?"

"Cindy wasn't available."

"You should have watched her better."

Jane couldn't deny the fact. "Accidents happen, Clarice. I agree, but this sort of thing happens to every mother at one time or another. Garrett showed me the scar on his hand where he cut himself making a sandwich when he was little. I'm sure that was an accident."

"His father was watching him."

Of course he was. Perfect mother Clarice would never have allowed her child to make his own sandwich.

"Sammy's fine. She doesn't mind all the attention she's getting. Heath will have to have surgery."

"You care more about those people than your own child."

"*Those people* have been very good to me

and my daughter, and yes, we do care about them."

"We're coming to see Sammy for ourselves. I want to be sure she's okay."

Jane resented the implication that she'd lied about the situation. "You'll have to stay in a hotel."

"We want to spend time with Sammy."

"You're welcome to see her."

"I'll let you know when to expect us."

Just what she needed. Clarice would focus on making her life miserable for the duration of the stay. Not to mention she had no idea how Sammy would respond to the grandparents she hadn't seen in a year. Well, she'd worry about that when she knew for sure that they were coming.

"I'm going to work harder and do everything Heath planned," Jane vowed when Val came by the following morning with breakfast.

"Don't be silly."

She wilted. Now Val thought she was being ridiculous.

"Jane, I mean this in the most loving of ways. Give it a rest. You're blaming yourself, and you need to stop. It's not anything you can change."

"I could have."

"Could you really? What if you'd taken Sammy home and Heath stumbled over his own feet?"

"He wouldn't have been hurt as badly."

"Do you know that for sure? Trying to keep the box from hitting her could have kept him from falling on something sharp. He could have broken his neck. They were halfway up the stairs."

"I made a bad choice."

"Well, get in line. We all did."

"He's not going to be able to get around. Do you realize how that's going to make him feel?"

"Heath will be okay. Our family will take care of him. Just as we'll help you take care of Sammy."

"I don't deserve you as a friend."

"Sure you do." Val tilted her head toward the cries coming from Sammy's room. "Your most important responsibility needs attention. Call if you need help today."

"I will. Will you let me know how Heath's doing?"

"Not if you're going to obsess over the situation." Val stopped at the door and smiled at her. "He was awake when Mom called this morning and said the pain meds have everything under control. He wants pajamas. He's not in love with those hospital gowns."

"Few people are," Jane said with a big smile. She didn't know why she'd been blessed with people like the Trueloves in her life, but she thanked God for putting them there.

TEN

Heath came home from the hospital on the same day the Holts called to say they were on their way. That news didn't thrill Jane, but she'd done everything possible to prepare herself for the onslaught of criticism she knew Clarice would provide.

She returned to work after a couple of days off. Sammy started figuring out how to play around the cast. While Jane helped Val prepare the wedding venue for a wedding on Saturday, Sammy stayed with the Truelove family.

Despite Jane's concerns that it was too much on her, Cindy welcomed the child back, insisting the two patients could comfort each other. Sammy took her books and toys to Heath, who was pretty much off his feet until the doctor put a walking cast on his leg. He could get around with the crutches but said it wasn't the easiest thing he'd ever done.

When they came to the house for lunch, Jane found Sammy banging her storybook against Heath's arm in an effort to wake him. "Sammy, no. Heath's resting," she said, swinging the child up into her arms.

He woke and offered her a sleepy smile. "It's okay. I told her to get her storybook and fell asleep before she got back. Let her stay. She's good company."

Jane lifted the child onto the arm of his chair. "I'm so sorry about this, Heath."

"It can't be helped."

"It could. Now both of you are in pain, and it's my fault."

"I'm not in pain," Heath said, pulling a bottle of pills from his shirt pocket and shaking them at her.

Horror filled Jane.

"What's wrong?"

"You can get addicted to those things."

"I only take them when the pain is really bad."

Jane reached for the bottle and read the label. "Garrett took those for his knee injury. He said he could stop anytime, but he couldn't."

Heath frowned. "I was only trying to lighten the mood. I'm not a pill taker. Never have been. I rarely take aspirin. I might be a little uncomfortable, but I'll survive. Sammy will, too."

Jane fingered her daughter's blond curls. "Please watch her around those pills."

He slipped them into the back of the table drawer under some papers. "When do you expect the Holts?"

"This afternoon." She found the idea depressing.

"It will be okay, Jane."

"I hope so."

Her in-laws hadn't been there an hour when Clarice started. "We want to take Sammy back to the hotel and spend time with her there."

Her grandmother held out her arms, but Sammy turned her head into Cindy True-love's neck. When she refused to let go, Clarice pulled her from Cindy's hold. Sammy sobbed.

"Is it necessary to upset her like this?" Cindy asked, dismayed by Sammy's distress.

"She's my granddaughter. I think I know what's best for her. She'll calm down once she's in the car."

Sammy's cries turned into screams as she reached out to the people she knew and loved. Jane stepped in and took her child from Clarice. "No. I'm not putting her through this. You can visit here, and if she becomes comfortable and wants to go with you later, we'll decide then."

"You can use the living room," Cindy volunteered.

"No," Clarice said. "I have gifts for her back at the hotel."

Jane rocked the child, smoothing her hair and whispering that it would be okay. "The gifts can wait. Thanks for the use of the room, Cindy."

The Trueloves left them to visit, all on alert for Sammy's cries.

"I can't believe you're treating us like this," Clarice told Jane.

"Can't you see she's scared? She hasn't seen you in a year and has no idea who you are. Give her time to adapt."

"She's certainly adapted to this family," Clarice sniped.

"Do you want to visit your granddaughter?" Jane asked, one breath away from ordering them to leave.

Edward Holt stepped forward. "She's right, Clarice. We need to give Sammy time to know us."

"It's a sad day when a grandmother can't hold her own grandchild," she mumbled angrily.

Garrett's dad sat by them on the sofa, talking softly to Sammy. Soon he caught the child's attention, and she lifted her tear-stained face to stare at him.

"What's wrong with Sammy?" Heath demanded when Val and his mom entered the family room.

"The Holts want to take her back to their hotel, and she's not having anything to do with them. Her grandmother tried to force the issue."

"Poor kid," he said. "This must be why Jane dreaded their visit."

Cindy glanced at Val and asked, "What do you think about offering the Holts a guest room? Sammy and Jane could stay, too. That might make things easier for Sammy."

"Good idea," Heath said enthusiastically. "Why don't you run it by Jane now and see what she thinks?"

"I'll ask after a while," Val said. "Let them have some time alone first."

After they left the room, Heath found himself listening for Sammy's cries. He didn't want her upset. Particularly since he knew her arm probably hurt as bad as his leg.

Much to Jane's dismay, the Holts accepted the invitation and arrived with luggage the next day.

"I appreciate your family suggesting we all stay here," Jane told Heath. "Sammy's more comfortable with me nearby."

"And you're more comfortable here, too?" Heath asked.

For the first time since she had become a Holt, Jane felt as if someone was on her side. She appreciated the Trueloves' sacrifice. Maybe things would have been different if her own parents had been there for her. Jane nodded. "There was no way I'd allow them to take Sammy off alone after yesterday. And going anywhere with Clarice would be like going to war. I can do no right as far as she's concerned. Having the family as a buffer helps."

"People can be like that," Heath said. "Particularly when they're angry or grieving."

"I didn't make Garrett's choice."

"Think about how you've blamed yourself for the accident. Don't you think Clarice wonders if she should have done something differently?"

Jane knew Heath tried to be the voice of reason but didn't believe Clarice would ever feel that she could have played a part in what happened to Garrett. It had been bad enough when Garrett was alive, but since his death, it had become intolerable. "No.

She's placed the blame solely on me. It's my fault. I drove her precious son to do what he did."

"I pray it stops."

"It had better. I'd hate to cut them off from Sammy, but I won't continue to tolerate Clarice's attacks either. I can't. It's very demoralizing to have someone tell you you're lousy at everything you do."

As the week passed, Heath could definitely understand Jane's frustrations. No matter what Jane said or did, Clarice belittled her. At times it got so bad that his mother sent Jane off to take a break while they babysat Sammy.

The child warmed up a little to her grandfather but kept her grandmother at arm's length. Instead of backing off and giving Sammy an opportunity to adapt, Clarice pushed even harder.

Sammy often played in the family room with Heath nearby in the recliner. That afternoon Clarice used his lack of mobility to move Sammy out of sight. He'd tried not to interfere, but when Sammy's screams reached him, Heath called Jane.

"I can hear," Jane said the moment she answered.

Sammy's shrieks became even louder. A

few seconds later she ran into the room and over to Heath. He dropped the phone and lifted her into his arms, holding her close and whispering soothing words. "Calm down, Sammy. It's okay." After she grew quieter, he picked up the receiver and said, "She's with me."

"I'm coming up there to talk to Clarice. This is ridiculous."

"I'll talk to her if you'd like." Heath had no idea what he could say to the woman, but he'd do what he could to help.

"Oh, I'd love to push that off on you, but I can't."

Deciding a confrontation was the last thing they needed, he said, "Finish your work, Jane. Sammy's okay. You can talk to Clarice later."

"Thanks, Heath."

Clarice entered the room. "Sammy, there you are. Why did you run away from Grandmother?" The way the child hid her face in Heath's chest made the woman even angrier. "Why do you keep interfering with my efforts to spend time with Sammy?"

"For the same reason you insist on forcing her to do something she doesn't want to do," Heath said, not bothering to temper the truth. "She's a child. Give her a chance to get to know you on her terms. All this chasing and dragging her off against her will only makes things worse."

Her sniff of disapproval spoke volumes. "What do you know about children?"

"I was one. I wouldn't have liked it either."

That gave Clarice pause. "So what do you suggest?"

"Sit down and have a conversation." Heath indicated the chair next to his. "Sit there. Maybe read us a story."

"Us?"

Heath grinned and raised his leg. "Sure. I'll listen. It's not like I'm going anywhere."

The next half hour proved to be interesting. Clarice actually did an excellent job of reading the story. "What do you think, Sammy?" Heath asked. "Pretty good, huh?"

Sammy's curls bobbed when she nodded. Her grandmother beamed.

"I used to volunteer for library story hours."

"You don't do it anymore?"

"Not since Garrett's . . ." She trailed off.

"You should. You're really good," Heath complimented. "You do great sound effects."

"I used to make up stories for Garrett. Every night before bed there was one. The ongoing story of Maxie Cat . . ."

"Why don't you tell us?"

She held up her hands. "Oh, I couldn't. Too many memories."

"I'm sure Sammy would like to hear the stories you told her dad."

Clarice began telling the story of Maxie, the fat white cat that liked to hang out in the trees with the birds. Sammy settled back against Heath's chest and soon drifted off.

"You think she's bored?"

He looked down at the little girl. "Jane said she's not sleeping well."

"Why didn't she tell me that?"

Heath shrugged. "Maybe because she knows how you'll react."

Clarice puffed up. "I have a right to know."

"I'm not trying to offend you, Mrs. Holt." He searched for a way to change the subject. "Have you ever considered writing a children's book? That's a very entertaining story. I really liked the part where he tried to fly when he scared the birds away."

"Garrett laughed so hard when I told that one," she said, her eyes filling with tears. "I don't have the heart for it anymore. Since Garrett's death, I haven't felt like doing anything."

"You have to find reasons to keep going," he said gently. "I'd say this one right here is mighty precious."

Clarice's gaze focused on Sammy. "She is.

Would you like me to take her?"

"She's okay. She gets grouchy if we wake her before her nap is over."

"I'm so thankful she wasn't hurt worse."

Her tiny cast rested on his arm, reminding Heath of their tumble. "Me, too. I did everything possible to keep from falling on her."

"How bad is your leg?"

"They put me back together with a plate and screws. Doctor says I'm young, and he expects a full recovery."

"This wouldn't have happened if Jane had —"

"Please don't finish that," Heath interrupted. "It wouldn't have happened if I'd looked before starting up the stairs with a big box blocking my view. I knew Sammy could be anywhere, and I didn't check."

"But Jane —"

"Is a good mother, Mrs. Holt. Accidents happen. There are too many kids out there with parents who don't care to criticize those who do."

Heath doubted she was ready to accept anything less than an error in judgment on Jane's part. He knew they were all at fault and each of them carried their own guilt.

"I think I'll go up and lie down for a

while. Something I ate isn't agreeing with me."

Heath hoped she didn't insult his mother and sister with that comment. Lunch had been delicious.

As Heath feared, the mood in the house didn't improve with the passing of time. That night at dinner, Sammy was whiny.

"Stop it, Samantha, or you'll go to bed now."

"Don't talk to her like that. She's tired," Clarice said from her seat across the table.

Jane looked at her and said, "I realize that. But I will not allow her to behave this way."

When Sammy flung her spoon with her good hand, Jane removed her from the high chair.

"No, Mommy!" she screamed when Jane asked everyone to excuse them.

"She's too hard on her," Clarice said to her husband.

Ed Holt continued to eat his dinner.

"The child needed discipline," Jacob said. "She's eaten at our table many times, and I've never known her to behave this way."

"She's overexcited. And in pain. Jane should know that."

"Why do you do that?" Heath demanded.

Clarice looked surprised. "Do what?"

He noted the way Clarice hid behind her innocent facade. He'd held his tongue for too long. Someone had to say something, or it would never stop. "You constantly criticize Jane."

"You're in love with her," Clarice accused, glaring at him.

"I consider her a good friend."

Clarice looked at her husband. "See. He knows better than to get tied up with her. He knows the kind of person she is. They went to school together."

Heath shook his head. "No. You don't understand. Jane doesn't deserve the way you treat her. No one does."

"She drove Garrett to do what he did."

Frustrated by her failure to understand, Heath hit his hands on the tabletop, raising his voice as he declared, "No, she didn't. We make our own decisions in life. When are you going to accept that she's still griev-ing, too? Maybe you should try putting the blame where it belongs. On your son."

"Garrett had a good future ahead of him before he got involved with her." Clarice's eyes became glassy and her voice more emotional. "And now that he's gone, he'll never know his daughter."

"Jane is carrying her own load of guilt, and you're only making things worse. As long as you blame her, you don't have to open your eyes and see your son had the real problem."

"Heath," his mother said.

He flashed her a repentant look as he said, "I'm sorry, but it needs to be said. They can help each other heal or destroy each other. Don't you want a relationship with your granddaughter?"

"Of course I want only the best for Sammy."

"Sammy is the most important person in Jane's life. She loves her a great deal and takes excellent care of her." The rest of his family nodded in agreement.

"She's got you all fooled. Just like she fooled Garrett."

"Jane is honest and sincere," Val defended. "She's genuine. Not at all deceptive."

Jane had carried Sammy into the family room to calm her down. She could hear their raised voices as the argument continued. This situation wasn't fair to the Trueloves who had done far too much for them already. She needed to take Sammy home, and the Holts could go back to a hotel.

The dinner soon broke up, and as the others left the dining room, Jane considered what she should do.

"Where's Horsie, Mommy?" Sammy asked sleepily.

Jules came into the room, and Jane asked her to watch Sammy while she retrieved the toy.

Heath still sat in his chair, staring idly out the window, when she walked in. "Sammy forgot Horsie," she said, picking up the stuffed animal from the buffet.

"Is she okay?"

"Tired and cranky, but she'll be fine. I heard what you told Clarice. Thanks for defending me, but you're wrong. I deceived my parents in my quest for popularity."

"I'm not judging you, Jane."

"I feel guilty, Heath. I let so many people down."

"You were blinded by love and needs far bigger than you realized at the time."

"What made you different? Why didn't you do the things Garrett did?"

"I knew God."

"I knew Him, too, but He wasn't my focus."

"That's what happens when we lose sight of God and the plans He has for us. He gave you free will, allowed you to make your own choices. And He's stood by you throughout it all, Jane."

"Why didn't He stop me?"

"Would you respect God more if He controlled you like a puppet?"

Jane shook her head.

"It's not a pick and choose kind of relationship. You can't live as you want and expect Him to keep you from making mistakes."

"I know. It's like Sammy getting hurt when I've warned her not to do something."

Heath nodded. "All you can do is comfort her and say you're sorry."

"God's like that, isn't He? When we're in the right relationship with Him, He sends comfort and soothes the pain."

"He is. So why did you separate yourself from His love?"

Jane shrugged. "I'm not known for making the best decisions."

"You could be. None of us knows what's best. You don't think I've had doubts? Part of me feels I should be out there earning a living with the education my family sacrificed to help me achieve."

"But another part wants the landscape job," Jane said slowly. Heath struggled with his choices as well. "Didn't you want the MBA?"

"Yes and no. If I get a good paying job and make the right decisions, I can do what

I really want to do — support my wife and family."

"You think maybe God redirected your path when He blessed Val with the funds?"

"I considered that. He certainly opened doors. I'd like to repay Val for what she's done for me. I want Your Wedding Place to become wildly successful."

"I know what you mean. I feel like she's gifted me time after time. Her generosity can be overwhelming."

Heath laughed. "She'd give you the clothes off her back if she thought you needed them. But in your case, you're help-ing each other. Val knows she can depend on you to get the job done. She's being a good employer when she provides you with benefits."

"All of you have been there for me lately. I can't even say that about my own parents."

"I believe God gives us what we need."

Jane nodded. She knew she should go home but couldn't bring herself to walk away from their support. "I pray He gives me the strength to get through this visit without doing harm to Clarice."

"He will," Heath promised.

"I'd better get back to Sammy. I asked Jules to keep an eye on her for a minute. She'll wonder what happened to me."

"Pray and believe, Jane. God will truly bless you. Just ask Val."

ELEVEN

Jane found when she did as Heath suggested that her prayers strengthened her throughout the Holts' stay. At times she thought she saw sympathy in Ed's eyes, but he never said anything about his wife's behavior. She couldn't say who was more relieved when Ed announced they would be leaving the next day.

After waving them off early Saturday morning, she packed their things, apologized to the Trueloves yet again, and moved back home. The Truelove home was wonderful, but the few days with Clarice made Jane long for the privacy of her own home.

They had a wedding on Saturday, and when Val gave her Monday off, Jane used the time to give her home a good cleaning. The papers on her nightstand reminded Jane to call the doctor's office. She dialed the number and said, "This is Jane Holt. I was sorting through my late husband's papers and came across a statement. Can you tell me why Garrett Holt was seeing Dr. Arnold?"

The woman paused. "I'm sorry, ma'am, but we're not allowed to give out information on patients without permission."

"But I'm his wife," Jane objected. "And he's deceased."

"Hold please, ma'am."

A couple of minutes later another woman came on the line. "Mrs. Holt, this is Geraldine Green. I will need to check your husband's file to see if he authorized us to share that information with you. We also need to verify you are his wife."

"Garrett is dead. He's been dead for more than a year now. He never mentioned seeing a Dr. Arnold."

"Ma'am, if you'll give me a number where you can be reached . . ."

Jane gave her the number. She understood they had a job to do, but she couldn't let confidentiality laws keep her from getting the answers she needed.

After finding her marriage license and Garrett's death certificate, Jane put Sammy in her car seat and drove to Lexington. The doctor was out of town, but the staff verified her identity, copied the papers, and promised to have the doctor contact her when he returned. Accepting she'd done all she could for now, Jane took Sammy grocery shopping and drove home.

It took a few days for the doctor's office to get back to her. She was shopping for antiques in Paris when her phone rang.

"Mrs. Holt, this is Dr. Arnold. My staff tells me you're inquiring about your husband's visits to my office."

"I'd like to know why he saw an oncologist. Garrett never indicated that he'd seen anyone other than his orthopedic specialist."

"According to our records, he came in for a second opinion. The diagnosis was stage-four pancreatic cancer. We concurred with the initial physician that his cancer was too far advanced to take any further actions."

Startled, Jane grabbed the back of a Chippendale chair she'd been admiring and held on. "Cancer?" Her eyes drifted closed as she drew several deep breaths.

"Yes. It's difficult when a man as young as your husband learns he has terminal cancer."

Why hadn't he told her? The idea that they had lived as man and wife and he'd kept this kind of information from her broke Jane's heart. "He committed suicide, Dr. Arnold."

"I'm sorry, Mrs. Holt. If he had come to see us earlier . . ."

The drinking. The drugs. Had depression over the news pushed him to this?

"Do you recall his state of mind regarding the diagnosis, Dr. Arnold?"

"I do remember your husband. I saw him play at UK. It really was a shame when he injured his knee. While I can't speak as to his frame of mind, I will say I've dealt with lots of cancer patients and most are shocked when they learn they only have a short time to live."

"How short?" she demanded.

Papers rustled, and he said, "I estimated Mr. Holt had three months."

Garrett must have been devastated. And so afraid. He hadn't been very brave when it came to the bad things in life. How could he keep that kind of secret and not turn to anyone for help? "Why wouldn't he tell me? His parents?"

She heard papers rustling again. "I'm afraid I can't say. I only saw him a few days before he died. May I ask why his death was ruled suicide?"

The images of that day were vivid. When she arrived home and couldn't wake Garrett, she'd called 911. Their efforts to revive him were futile. "When we found him, there was an empty pill bottle and liquor."

"If there was no weapon involved, I would wonder if his pain-management techniques caused problems. He was on a strong medication that doesn't respond well to alcohol."

"Are you saying it could have been an accidental overdose?"

"He would have been in a great deal of pain, and he could have confused his medication times and overmedicated himself."

"I thought the pain medication was for his knee injury." She paused, mulling over an idea that had just occurred to her. "Dr. Arnold, is it possible to amend a death certificate? I'm sure his parents would like to know, and I know I would, particularly for our daughter's sake. I don't look forward to telling her what happened to her father when she's older."

"You can appeal through the county coroner or state medical examiner. Have your attorney contact me, and we'll discuss the matter further."

She couldn't afford an attorney. She had a little saved since working with Val, but that was for their future. "My husband's death left me with expenses that pretty much take every dime of my income."

"I understand, Mrs. Holt. Talk with your family. If I can be of assistance to you in the future, feel free to contact me."

"Thank you."

Another wrong assumption, Jane thought. Granted, experts had agreed, but maybe if she'd been a better wife, more open to the truth rather than frustrated and angry with Garrett because he wasn't accepting his responsibility, he might have told her. She wept. Huge tears flowed for the loved one cancer had claimed.

Randi Cole, an acquaintance from high school who now owned the antique store, came to where she stood. "Jane, are you okay?"

"I'm sorry. I need to go."

Lost in a maelstrom of guilt and grief, Jane sat in the truck. She had no idea how much time had passed when Heath tapped on the passenger side window. She couldn't look at him as she released the lock, and he swung himself inside.

"Randi called the house. She's worried about you. What happened?"

"I'm sorry." The words came out in a croak. "The doctor called." The tears returned.

"Jane? Talk to me. Are you sick?"

His obvious anxiety forced her to respond. "No. Garrett had cancer. He never told me."

Heath slipped his arm around her shoulders. "How did you find out?"

"I discovered a bill from an oncologist while sorting his personal papers. He had stage-four pancreatic cancer."

When Heath wrapped her in his arms, she went willingly. "It hurts so much that he didn't tell me. The doctor said he only saw him days before he died."

"Maybe he thought it best not to fight the disease and was afraid you wouldn't agree."

What if Heath was right? Did that mean Garrett hadn't considered being there for her and Sammy sufficient reason to fight the illness? "The doctor said he would have been in a great deal of pain. I was working so much, and now that I look back, there were nights when Garrett was already in bed when I got home from work with Sammy. It drove me crazy that he couldn't be bothered to spend time with his family. Now I realize he was sick."

"Don't blame yourself, Jane. You couldn't know."

"I should have known," she said.

"Let's get you home."

"I should apologize to Randi."

"You can call her tomorrow. I want you to ride with me and Jim."

"But the truck —"

"We brought Glenn." Heath named two of the security staff who now worked at the farm. "He'll drive the truck home."

Jane didn't argue. She was in no shape to drive anywhere. A few minutes later she sat in the backseat of the SUV, Heath's arm about her shoulders. "Thanks for coming."

"You can always count on me, Jane."

At the farm Heath suggested that she take some time for herself. He promised to bring Sammy home after dinner. Afraid her state of confusion would upset her daughter, Jane agreed, and Heath took time to pray with her before she left the vehicle.

A couple of hours later Jane had cried herself dry and forced herself to look at the situation objectively. What could she do to turn this around for Sammy? If she pursued the matter, would they find it had been an accident? Money held her back. She couldn't afford to invest her savings in what could be a futile venture.

Heath and Val brought Sammy home around 8:00 p.m. "She's bathed and changed into her pj's," Val said as the child reached for her mother. "Everyone says to tell you that you're in their prayers."

Jane hugged Sammy close and smiled at them. "Thank you," she mouthed.

Heath rested his hand on her arm. "Are you okay?"

She nodded. "Let me put her down, and we'll talk."

Jane read Sammy a story, and she drifted off to sleep. Jane doubted sleep would come as easily for her that night.

When she walked into the living room, Heath hit the remote and turned off the TV. "Val said to tell you she'd check in with you later."

Jane nodded. "Thanks for all you've done. I wasn't in any shape to keep her earlier."

"I can take her back to the house if you need more time."

"No. We'll be okay. I was so upset that I didn't tell you everything. The doctor thinks it's possible Garrett's death wasn't suicide." She told him what the man had said. "I'd like to clear his name for his parents and Sammy."

"What about you?" Heath asked as he took her hand in his.

"I'm at peace with what I've learned." The moment the words left her lips, Jane realized that she did feel relieved. She attributed it to the prayers offered up in her time of need. "Thinking it could have been a mistake makes the situation more tolerable. The doctor said there's an appeal process with new evidence. He said he would talk to my lawyer, but I told him I couldn't afford legal assistance."

"Would you like me to help?"

She smiled and shook her head. She refused to take advantage of him in yet another way. "I'll tell Garrett's parents. If they want to pursue the matter, they certainly have funds to do so."

"Do you think it will change Clarice's outlook toward you?"

"I doubt it. She'll only wonder what I did to Garrett to make him not tell me."

"He must not have told her either."

Jane flashed him a wry smile. "Maybe that will make a difference."

Heath woke early the following morning, determined to do something productive with his day. He convinced Roc to bring a shovel and a tray of asters out to the front yard before leaving for school. After several failed attempts at working around his disability, he became frustrated.

"You're going to hurt yourself worse," Jane said when she found him trying to balance on crutches and work a shovel. "Tell me what you're trying to do."

"I want to plant those bulbs over here."

"What else?"

She listened as he outlined the things he wanted done. Jane found him a chair and placed it in the shade before she started work.

"There," she said, patting the soil about the transplanted bulbs. "Is that what you wanted?"

He stood and swung himself over to take a look. The crutch pushed into the soft ground, and he nearly toppled. Jane jumped up and grabbed his arm.

Disgusted with himself, Heath jumped back on more solid ground. "Yeah, that's good. If you get me a pair of clippers, I can sit down and work on these low shrubs."

They worked in silence until Heath needed to move on to the next shrub. Each time, she repositioned his seat and made certain he had everything he needed before returning to her task. By lunchtime Heath accepted that he was more of a hindrance than a help. "I'm sorry, Jane. I've been so preoccupied with myself that I didn't even ask how you were feeling this morning."

Jane stopped to pull a weed from the bed next to the house. "I'm okay. Still working through a few issues in my mind, but at least yesterday's news gave me hope where there was none."

"Hope?"

"For Sammy. One day she'll ask about her dad. It would be better to say his death was accidental rather than intentional."

Heath understood why she'd want that for her daughter.

"You want to go to the antique store with me this afternoon?" Jane asked as they entered the house. "I called Randi earlier, and she said they received some things they think Val would like."

"Might as well. I'm useless on the land-scaping until this comes off. We could take Sammy along."

"To an antique store?"

He grinned. "I see your point."

Heath soon realized things weren't going to be any better for him at the store. Navigating the antique-filled room on crutches would be impossible. "Why don't I sit here while you take a look at the items?"

"What if we bring them to you?"

"That would work."

Randi Cole helped Jane with a mantel clock she thought the Trueloves might like. Heath agreed, and they bought the clock, a silver sugar and creamer set, and a pair of candlesticks.

While Randi wrote up the order, Jane looked down into the display case and gasped. "Can I please see that garnet ring?"

Randi slid the door open and pulled out the tray. "We just got these in last week."

"It's my birthstone."

"When is your birthday?" Heath asked.

"January 31st."

The ring fit perfectly. He noted the way she twisted her hand from side to side, enjoying the play of light on the beautiful stone. "You should buy it."

Her gaze shifted to the ring and back to him before she sighed and slipped it off, laying it back on the tray.

"Another time, maybe." She picked up the few items Randi had wrapped for her and said, "I'll put these in the truck and come back for the clock."

Randi called out to her husband then said to Jane, "David can take that out for you."

The chimes over the door rang as they went out.

Heath did a one-legged dance as he got to his feet and shoved the crutches under his arms. He moved over to the counter. "I want to buy that ring."

Randi smiled. "She'll love your gift."

Heath pulled his wallet from his pocket and handed the woman a bill, pushing his change and the receipt back inside the wallet before he pocketed the ring.

Randi came around the counter and held the door open for him. "How long before you get that off?"

"Soon, I hope." He winked down at her. "Thanks for your help. Have a good day."

Heath moved down to where the sidewalk dipped for wheelchair access and into the parking lot. Jane had the extended cab door open as she placed the items in the back. She opened Heath's door for him. "I think Val will like those candlesticks. She wanted a set for the fireplace mantel."

"It's great that they know what we're looking for," Heath said.

"I appreciate all the help I can get. Ready to go home?"

He leaned up against the truck and pulled the bag from his pocket. "I bought you something."

Jane frowned.

Heath pushed the bag in her direction. "Here, take it."

"You can't buy that," she protested when she removed the ring.

"Why not? You bought me a gift."

"Yeah, but . . ."

"No buts. Do unto others."

She slipped it on her finger and held out her hand, admiring the gorgeous ring. Jane turned and threw her arms around his neck, almost unbalancing them both with her exuberance. "Thank you!"

"Hey, Jane, we're going to a UK football game," Opie said over the phone. "Want to come?"

Memories washed over Jane. She'd spent hours too numerous to count in Commonwealth Stadium, cheering Garrett on, play after play. Seeing happiness in his expression that she never saw when they were alone together.

"Jane?"

"I'm here. I don't know if I can."

"You already have plans?" she asked.

"No. Too many memories."

"Oh. I hadn't considered that."

Maybe it would be good for her to go back again. Make new memories with new friends. "Who's going?"

"Heath, Val, me, and you if you want. A client gave Russ the tickets. We're meeting him and Rom."

"I need to find a babysitter."

"Mom said you can bring Sammy over."

"What time?"

"We're leaving in an hour."

"I'll be there."

Opie paused. "Jane, you don't have to do this."

"I want to. See you soon."

Later, as they followed crowds of students, fans, staff, and alumni into Commonwealth Stadium, Jane couldn't help but wonder why she'd agreed to this. The idea of enjoying herself with new friends warred with the fear that she could be a wet blanket and ruin the outing.

They picked up Russ and Rom at the apartment, and Jim dropped them off at the entrance. Jane smiled when Val and Opie jostled each other like playful puppies. They would root for UK, but win or lose it was all about fun. Once they arrived at their seats, Jane ended up next to Heath. That was more than okay with her.

Things weren't as bad as she had feared. From the kickoff, Jane quickly got into the game.

"Go, Cats!" Jane shouted, pumping her arm in the air when they scored their first touchdown. Fireworks shot from atop the scoreboard.

"Having fun?" Heath asked, grinning at her enthusiastic high fives to the others.

The Wildcats were ahead at halftime when the championship cheerleading team came on the field. She watched their routine with interest.

"Did you try out for the squad?" Heath asked.

Jane's heart had been so burdened by grief that she'd never considered trying out. She shook her head.

The game resumed with the home team managing to maintain their lead. In the fourth quarter, the quarterback raced down the field, the ball clutched in his arms. How many times had she watched Garrett run exactly like this kid, confident, taunting them as he nimbly dodged their grabbing hands and charging bodies? Just when she thought he might make it, the kid went down under the pile of players. When they rolled away, he writhed in agony, clutching his knee.

Jane shot to her feet. "Do something," she called as if they could hear. "He's hurt."

Heath stood, his arm going around her waist. "Shh. It's okay. See, they're helping him."

She couldn't look. Jane knew she had to escape. She looked at Heath and implored, "Let's get out of here. Please."

"Want to take a walk?" Heath asked.

Jane nodded.

"We'll meet you guys out front."

As Jane fled the stadium, Heath followed at a much slower pace. "Hey, slow down," he called.

Seeing that young man down took Jane back to the incident she considered the downfall of her marriage. It still hurt that football made Garrett happier than being married to her. "I'm sorry." She spotted a bench over to the side. "We can sit over there."

"Are you okay?"

Embarrassed by her reaction, Jane looked down. "Better. You probably recall I'm a wimp when it comes to someone getting hurt."

"You were enjoying the game."

She nodded. "I always enjoyed football. In high school, people saw the perky cheerleader on the sidelines, but I understood the plays. When I asked Garrett why they didn't try a new play, he listened. I think he made the coaches think they were his ideas. I should have joined a sport, but I stayed with cheerleading. My mom thought that was more feminine. She didn't want her daughter to become a female jock."

"You're no jock," Heath said. "Why didn't you join the cheerleading squad at UK?"

She shrugged. "I didn't have the heart for it anymore."

As their conversation veered toward the campus that had been a part of their lives,

Jane said, "Seems like a million years ago."

"I didn't get to a lot of games. Rom and I lived at home and drove to classes."

"Not your usual college experience. Did you miss living on campus?"

"The education was more important. That degree opens the door to opportunities."

Jane realized he hadn't seen college as a means of escape from his parents and family. He'd set his priorities and gone after what he considered to be important, all the while considering the people he loved most. "What about your résumé? How will helping Val affect that?"

"Working for the family business," Heath said. "Write enough technical jargon, and it fits."

"Particularly when your sister is a multi-millionaire," Jane agreed. "So you don't plan to landscape forever?"

"I probably will in some way, but it won't be my job. When we finish up Val's plans, I'll find a position like Rom's."

Jane knew Heath would set another priority and sacrifice his happiness because he thought it was the right thing to do. "You could make a living designing and installing landscapes."

"I've thought about it," Heath admitted. "More than a time or two."

Jane smiled at him. "You'll make the right decision."

TWELVE

Heath lay on the sofa flipping through the television channels. In the weeks since the accident he'd been unable to help in the gardens.

"You're looking glum," Val said as she walked into the family room.

"I'm over doing nothing."

"There's not much you can do at this point," she reminded him.

"I know. I was thinking about visiting My Old Kentucky Home."

"Are you up to walking that much?"

Heath shrugged. "You mentioned a country garden recently, and that struck me as a place that would offer some good ideas. I figured I could find places to rest when I need to."

"Jim could drive you."

Heath shook his head. They had hired the driver/bodyguard to transport the women in the family to wherever they needed to go.

He wasn't about to leave them stranded while he went sightseeing. "He needs to stick around here."

"What about Jane? I can spare her if you think she'd like to go."

Things hadn't been the same between them since his dad's birthday. Maybe spending some time together would help them both overcome the situation. "I suppose we could ask."

A couple of minutes later, Val laughed as she slid her phone back into her pocket. "Given how quickly she said yes, Jane must really want to go."

"Probably thinks it's the least that she can do. She keeps apologizing."

"I've heard you apologize to Sammy more than once," Val said.

He nodded. "It's a vicious circle. Guilt is a terrible thing."

"I know. I told Jane you'd meet her at the truck."

"Thanks. I'd better tell Opie we won't be around for lunch."

"I'll do that."

"Thanks, Val." Heath grabbed his crutches and started out the door. He paused. "You want to come with us?"

"Not today. Have fun but don't overdo."

Jane echoed Val's sentiments a few minutes later when he approached the vehicle. "Are you sure you're up to this?"

"I'm going crazy sitting in the house."

She opened his door and gestured him in. Once inside she took his crutches and placed them in the backseat. Jane went around and climbed into the driver's seat. "What's the plan?"

"My Old Kentucky Home."

She looked baffled. "I thought you'd lived here at Sheridan Farm all your life."

"Not mine. Federal Hill in Bardstown. It's where Stephen Foster wrote the song when he visited his family."

"Oh, *that* Old Kentucky Home," Jane said. "Never been there."

"I'll put the address in the GPS," Heath told her. "Val says after you get past being freaked out because this box knows your every move, you love it."

"Must have been created by a man who hated asking for directions."

"It's a woman giving the directions," Heath said, grinning when he added, "I figure some poor wife couldn't stand the arguments and created the thing for her poor misguided husband."

Jane started the vehicle and put it into Drive. She laughed when the woman's voice directed her to turn right. "So why did you choose My Old Kentucky Home?"

"I wanted to check out the grounds."

"Sounds like a lot of walking."

Jane's dubious expression made him wonder if he'd made the right decision. "I'll have to take breaks, but it beats sitting around home all day."

"I'm . . ."

"Don't say it. In fact, don't even think it," he ordered.

"But you're frustrated, and I'm sorry."

"It's not your fault," Heath said.

"I should have taken Sammy upstairs with me."

"Life isn't in our control, Jane. We both learned valuable lessons. I learned it's not smart to carry boxes that block your view up the stairs. At least not before making certain the path is clear. Sammy learned not to play on the stairs."

"And to watch out for big men carrying boxes," Jane said.

He nodded. "We're not used to having little people around. We'll have to pay closer attention to keep her protected."

"I'm used to doing it alone."

"Now you have a village. Why not use it?"

"I trust Sammy with your family, Heath. I'm thankful for all you've done for us both. Val paid the hospital bill. She said she couldn't believe she hadn't thought about health insurance benefits for us." She was silent for a few minutes. "What kind of garden is Val considering now?"

"She mentioned a country garden. We'll look at what they have, and then I thought we'd check out Bernheim Arboretum and have lunch at the tavern in Bardstown."

"Okay, but promise to tell me when it gets to be too much?"

Heath nodded. The trip went quickly as they discussed the gardens at Sheridan Farm. She parked and went around the truck to help. "They might have a wheelchair."

Shaking his head, Heath placed his crutches underneath his arms. No way would he force her to push him around in a wheelchair. "I've got it under control."

Inside, Heath gave her money for the tour tickets. They walked past the family cemetery and down pathways leading toward Federal Hill.

"Stephen Foster wrote the state song, 'My Old Kentucky Home,' while visiting his cousins back in 1852. I'm going to give the house tour a miss." When Jane looked longingly at the house, he said, "You go ahead. I'll meet you out back in the gardens."

While he waited, Heath found a bench

and enjoyed the music playing over a speaker. He watched as people decorated the pergola for a wedding and realized Val's structure would be pretty much the same, only on a grander scale. When Jane exited the back door of the house, he came over to where she viewed what had been the house's kitchen.

"Has Opie seen this?"

He nodded. A fireplace was the room's focus along with a couple of tables. "Can't imagine her cooking in a place like this. Her idea of roughing it is using an electric hand mixer and can opener."

"Then she'd really hate this kitchen. No modern conveniences."

"I wonder if she'd find cooking as interesting without those things."

"Oh, I think so," Jane said. "Opie loves to cook." As they moved on, Jane said, "Life was much simpler then. The size of the house surprises me. The guide talked about the guests they had. Where did they put them? There are only three bedrooms."

"I read the house originally had thirteen rooms. Supposedly thirteen is repeated throughout the house to honor the thirteen colonies. Thirteen windows on the front, thirteen steps to each floor. Plus I think the families shared beds back then," Heath said.

"You should be a tour guide."

As they moved through the gardens, Heath asked, "Think we could re-create this at home?"

"Why would we want to?" Jane asked. "I mean they're nice, but the gardens we already have are exquisite."

"Val thought we might have brides who wanted something simpler."

"I doubt that bride would come to Sheridan Farm. She'd get married in someone's home garden and save her money."

Heath listened as Jane shared her thoughts.

"People expect spectacular for the money Your Wedding Place charges. You could set up chairs in the front yard and have what you have here. If you want to grow Your Wedding Place, add an atrium. A butterfly garden. A secret garden, even."

"You should suggest those to Val."

Jane turned away. "She knows what she wants."

Heath wondered at Jane's reluctance to share her opinion. Her outspokenness on so many levels made it seem strange. "I'm sure she'd appreciate your opinion."

"I'm no expert."

"You're a woman. A potential bride. You know what you'd choose."

"I'd never be able to afford one of Val's venues."

Heath laughed at that. "Me either, but knowing Val, she'd do it gratis or at least give us the employee rate."

"Do we have an employee rate?" Jane shrugged. "And since I'm not getting married, it's a moot point anyway."

"Would you like to be married again?"

"Are you asking?"

He knew her question embarrassed her when she quickly added, "Just kidding." The color rose in her cheeks. "Actually, when marriage is good, there's nothing better. Having someone who loves and cares for you is wonderful."

"I hope to find my soul mate and settle down. I feel like my life is on hold until I do."

"Don't rush things. If you manage to get the cart in front of the horse as I did, you give yourself unnecessary grief. My hope for the future is to find a man who loves Sammy and me as we deserve to be loved. Next time I'll find a man who knows where he's headed in life."

Her words hit Heath. Did she see what he was doing now as playing around with the future?

Sure, he enjoyed his work, but what did

he have beyond the money Val had given him for graduation and the weekly paychecks? Maybe more than some men but definitely no career plans.

"Not that I don't believe everyone has the right to make the decisions that affect their future," Jane added. "But he needs to have a plan in mind. Even if he's not established, he should know what he wants to do with his life."

"Do you have a plan?"

Jane shrugged. "I've thought about having a business to support Sammy and me. I'm putting away a little money every pay period. Val pays me well, and not having housing expenses helps."

"What kind of business?"

"The coffee shop is all I know. I suppose I could do that."

"You can do whatever you put your mind to, Jane. You're a dedicated worker. People recognize that about you."

"I hope so. I'm tired of making bad impressions."

"You never did that."

"Ask my parents or my in-laws. They'll tell you differently."

"There's only one judge who counts, Jane."

"Then I'm really in trouble."

He shook his head. "Sometimes when you get so far from God, you think you can't find your way back. He's right where He's always been."

"Your God, maybe."

"Yours. Mine. There's no difference. He's waiting for your return."

"And I'm trying to find my way back. I suppose the main thing I'm looking for in a future husband is not a plan but a desire to accomplish something worthwhile with his life."

Responsibility. Heath knew the feeling well. His brother's keeper. People had to help one another.

"A small gazebo like this one would be nice for brides with small parties," Jane said.

"You should tell Val. The secret garden is good, too. A private walled area could be a good addition."

Heath was glad to get back to the truck. "Let's just drive through Bernheim. I'm having muscle spasms from walking so much."

"Do we need to go home?"

"No. I just need to get off my leg."

He set the GPS for Bernheim and leaned back in the passenger seat.

"How's the leg?" Jane asked a few minutes later.

"Better. My bones are protesting because I'm making them work today instead of lying around the house."

Jane chuckled. "Let's hope they don't go on strike. Tell me where we're headed."

Since his injury, Heath had done a lot of reading and research. He remembered the area from a previous visit. "We're going to see nature as God intended. Isaac W. Bernheim established the Bernheim Arboretum and Research Forest back in 1929 to be used as a park. Fourteen thousand acres. It's been years in the development. There are hiking trails, lakes, wildlife, the arboretum, art. So much we're not going to see in a drive through."

"Maybe we can come back and spend more time after your cast comes off."

"Let's plan on that." He'd love to spend time hiking and connecting with Jane. She enjoyed the outdoors as much as he did, and Heath suspected she'd enjoy spending time in the beautiful natural setting.

After paying their admission fee, she drove the circular route through the park. Several times they stopped to study the sculpture collection along the way.

"People use the area for business and

educational meetings. Val could increase her profit margin by doing retreats," Heath said.

"The wedding venues are her focus for now, but as she becomes more comfortable, I think she'll branch out into other events."

"Baby steps," Heath said with a nod. "Makes sense."

They drove back into Bardstown for lunch at The Old Talbott Tavern. Choosing Kentucky Hot Brown from the menu, they enjoyed the open-face turkey sandwiches with bacon, parmesan cheese, and Mornay sauce. Heath shared about the historic old tavern and how it was said to be the oldest western stagecoach stop in America when the westward expansion brought explorers from the east into Kentucky.

"It's a bed-and-breakfast, too. We gave Mom and Dad a couple of nights in the Lincoln Suite for their anniversary last year. Mom loved it. Dad liked the My Old Kentucky Dinner Train." Heath's phone rang. "Excuse me."

A couple of minutes later, he slid the phone back into his pocket and said, "That was Val. Wanted to know when we'd be home."

"Why? Is Sammy okay?"

"She said everyone's fine. Maybe she's just checking up on me." Something told him there was more to it than that.

"Let's go," Jane said, sounding frightened.

Silence stretched on the trip home as they tried to understand what could have happened.

"Hef. Mommy," Sammy cried, jumping to her feet and racing across the room when Jane entered the Trueloves' kitchen. Jane allowed herself the luxury of a lengthy hug.

"What happened?" Heath asked.

"A process server came by to see Jane," Val said. "He left his card with security. I figured the sooner she knew, the better. Do you have any idea what's going on?"

Jane shook her head. She didn't have a clue. Taking the card, she swung Sammy up into her arms. "I intend to find out."

But no one answered when she called. She left a message on voice mail and then spent the evening wondering what was going on. Nothing came to mind. It couldn't be debt collection. Jane knew she wasn't behind on any of her bills. She'd committed no illegal acts. She hadn't done anything to be sued over.

Still full from her late lunch with Heath, Jane called the Trueloves to tell them she and Sammy wouldn't be coming over for dinner. She prepared Sammy's meal and played with her before putting her to bed.

Frustration over the situation and thoughts of the day she'd spent with Heath made Jane more miserable. Every minute spent in his company only made her want what she couldn't have. Finally, in desperation she picked up her Bible and started to read. She soon read Matthew 6:34: "Therefore do not worry about tomorrow, for tomorrow will worry about itself. Each day has enough trouble of its own." No matter how she worried about the legal issue or Heath's feelings for her, worrying wouldn't resolve either concern.

"I'm sorry, heavenly Father," she whispered. "Shamed that I made the decisions that separated me from You. I know You've been there, looking out for Sammy and me, giving us wonderful, loving friends like the Truelove family and providing for our needs. Please forgive my sins, and help me to find my answers in You. Dear God, help me to handle this situation. Please send Your peace and comfort, and thank You for giving me this chance to come home. Amen."

A smile touched her lips as she turned the lamp off and closed her eyes. God was with her. She could feel His presence.

The man delivered the papers early the following morning. When security called the house, Val and Heath walked out into the yard with her to meet him. Jane ripped open the envelope and read the document. Hurt turned her bones to mush. "The Holts have made good on their threat to file for custody."

Heath read the papers she handed him. "We need an attorney," he declared. "Val can get a referral from Mr. Henderson. They can't take Sammy from you."

"I don't have money for an attorney," Jane said, her feelings of hopelessness multiplying.

"I do."

She stared up at him. "I can't let you do that."

"You have to," Heath said. "If we don't do something, they could convince a judge to take your daughter. We have to act, and we need to do it now."

"That money is for your future."

Heath spread his hands wide, inviting her in, and said, "Don't you get it, Jane? I don't care about the money. I care about you and Sammy. I don't want to take chances."

Tears clogged her throat as she went into his arms for comfort.

Heath went with her to see the attorney Mr.

Henderson recommended. Val had attended high school with J. Paul Garner. After law school, he returned to Paris to set up his practice. His high success rate in the courtroom was good enough for her.

She hated feeling so emotional, so out of control. Sammy didn't know what to make of her clingy, weepy mother. The Trueloves tried to reassure her, but with all the other bad things that had happened in her life, she feared yet another nightmare. She had told Heath that on the drive to Paris.

"No judge is going to take a child away from their mother," Heath told her once again. "Tell her that, Paul."

Paul leaned back in his big chair. "Don't believe that, Heath. If Clarice Holt convinces a judge that being with Jane is not in Sammy's best interests, she could succeed."

"She will not take my child." Jane spoke with determination.

"We'll do everything possible to keep that from happening." Paul looked down at the paper on his desk. "She alleges that improper supervision resulted in your child's injury and that you left your injured daughter with a stranger while you went on dates with Heath Truelove."

Confused, Jane looked at Heath and back at Paul. "Why would she say that? When did she claim this happened?"

He checked the paper and indicated the dates and times.

"Part of my job is shopping for antiques for Val. Heath hasn't been able to work since hurting his leg and accompanied me a time or two. As for the day trip into Bardstown, we were researching garden ideas for Your Wedding Place."

"Mrs. Holt has photos of you hugging Mr. Truelove on the street in downtown Paris."

Jane couldn't believe what she was hearing. "She had me followed?"

"Why would hugging me make her a bad mother?" Heath demanded.

"Yes. That's how she got the photos," Paul told Jane. "And your relationship doesn't make her a bad mother," he said to Heath. "Evidently Clarice Holt has sufficient documentation to convince a judge to consider her case. We can't take anything for granted. Do you remember the incident?"

"Your ring," Heath said finally. "You hugged me that day."

Jane nodded. "Heath gifted me with a ring I admired in the store, and I hugged and thanked him. How could Clarice turn an innocent action into something so wrong? Sammy was with Heath's mother. Cindy Truelove cares for her while I work."

"Your mother-in-law also claims you're working all the time and not spending any time with Sammy. She says you weren't paying attention to your child the day her arm was broken."

Jane became more upset with each accusation. "My mother-in-law doesn't like me. She's made these outrageous claims ever since I married her son. Why is she making a big deal over Sammy spending time with others now? When I was the sole breadwinner for our family, Garrett didn't care for Sammy. She went to day care. I see her much more during the day with this job than when I worked at the coffee shop. I spend more quality time with her now than ever before."

"I'd advise you to let the investigators see for themselves that Clarice Holt doesn't like you. Hearing you say it makes it sound like an attempt to gain sympathy. I assume you have people who can attest to the type of mother you are?"

Heath leaned forward. "I can tell you she's wonderful with Sammy."

"We need others," the lawyer said. "The judge will feel that you're biased because of your alleged relationship with Jane."

"You mean our friendship?"

"Others may perceive it as more of a

romantic relationship given the hug that was witnessed by the private investigator."

"She's grieving for Garrett. That's the reason she's doing this. She wants his child."

"We're going to do everything possible to keep Sammy with you. The judge will make his decision based on the best interests of the child and who can provide the most stable environment for her. I suggest you start making lists. The time you spend with Sammy on a daily basis. People who have witnessed you interacting with her."

When she worked long hours at the coffee shop, Jane picked Sammy up and took her home. Their quality time involved getting the child fed, bathed, and into bed. Other than the occasional visit with the staff when she picked up her check on a day off, she really had no witnesses as to the type of mother she was. The day care staff had seen her with Sammy for brief periods each day. Only the Truelove family saw her with Sammy on a daily basis.

"Does our relationship disqualify my entire family?" Heath asked.

"No," Paul said with a shake of his head. "Of course not. Val is Jane's employer. Your mother is her day care provider. But we need others who have seen Jane interact with Sammy."

Heath looked at her and said, "People at church have seen you with her."

"They've seen me discipline her for yelling." Jane cringed at the thought. What if someone thought she was awful for doing that?

"And they know she was excited to see her mommy. I'm sure they could attest to what a good relationship the two of you have. Sammy is an active, healthy, normal two-year-old. They won't take her away from you."

"I wish I were as sure. Clarice and Ed have money. They can give her a better life than I can."

"They can't love her more than you do. Life isn't about possessions. Sammy has a good home, and you have a good support system in place. We're going to do everything possible to help you, Jane," Heath promised.

"Why does Clarice hate me so much that she'd want to take my child?"

"You saw how Sammy acted when they visited. I'm sure she wants to change that and thinks she can do so by having her closer."

"Church is good," Paul said. "Any extracurricular activities?"

"Her dance classes," Heath said. "They

see the two of you together when you take her for those."

Paul nodded again. "You need to think of anything and everything you can to help prove your parental capabilities. The broken arm . . ."

"It was an accident," Jane told him.

"The judge will listen. There's no history of Sammy injuring herself in other ways, is there?"

"She's an active child and has her share of bumps and bruises when she does things she's told not to do."

Paul grinned. "I have a two-year-old myself. I know how they can be."

"I didn't realize you had a child," Heath said.

"Denise and I got married before law school. We decided we didn't want to wait to start our family. She teaches at our church's Christian academy." He turned back to Jane. "What sort of relationship have your in-laws had with Sammy?"

"They lived here when she was a baby. They left almost a year ago, after Garrett's death. It's been telephone only since then."

"How do you feel about bringing Garrett's suicide up in court?"

"I don't like talking about it, but if it's what I need to do to hold on to my daughter, I will. You should know Clarice blames me for that, too. She claims I drove Garrett to suicide."

"Why would she say that?"

Jane shrugged, shaking her head. She'd spent years trying to understand the Holt family and was no closer than when she first started. "I worked twelve-hour shifts and took care of my child and home. He managed to get himself fired from every job he found and partied with his fraternity friends. I didn't have time to analyze Garrett's reasons for lots of things he did."

"You need to be careful with statements like that. They could reflect negatively on you."

Jane didn't understand. "Why would I look bad? I supported our family."

"Clarice Holt will come across as a grieving mother."

And she'd play the role to the hilt. Jane had no doubt that would be Clarice's first line of defense in this case. She would do everything possible to make Jane look bad. "I should tell you that I recently learned Garrett had terminal cancer. The doctor suggested the possibility that his death may have been accidental. He's willing to discuss it with an attorney, but I don't have funds to pursue the matter."

"Do the Holts know this?" Paul asked.

"No. I haven't told them. I planned to, but this situation has taken priority in my life."

"One case at a time. What can you tell me about your in-laws?"

"I can attest to how Clarice chased after Sammy when the child wanted nothing to do with her," Heath said. "And how she constantly demeans Jane." He looked at her and said, "We all saw how she treated you that week and need to make sure the judge knows as well."

The lawyer looked interested. "How do you know this?"

Heath explained the situation.

"In Sammy's defense, she hadn't seen her grandmother for a year," Jane said.

"She was very demanding," Heath added. "Seemed to think being alone with Sammy would change their relationship faster. Sammy's screams could be heard all over the house."

"Write it all down," Paul said. "I need to know what you know. I'll call as soon as I have more information."

Throughout the next day Jane could think of little more than Clarice's accusations and the pending court case. She had never been

the insecure type, but she had never considered having to prove herself a good mother.
When had loving and providing for your
child's needs stopped being enough? She
didn't plan to go down without a fight.
Clarice would not raise her daughter.

The Trueloves were very supportive and
had prayed for her and promised to do
everything possible to help. Jane felt better
knowing they were there for her.

She prayed her anger would subside before
she did or said something she would regret.
How dare Clarice have her followed like a
criminal, gathering evidence to convict her?
And why couldn't she hug a man? She
wasn't cheating on her husband.

Jane considered phoning Clarice but knew
they would only end up arguing, which
would reflect badly on her when the case
came to court. Ed's sympathetic looks came
to mind. Most of what she'd heard had been
Clarice. Could she reach Ed? Or would he
stand by his wife? The thought he could be
her only hope refused to be silenced. "Val, I
need to make a phone call."

"Go ahead."

Jane found her address book and looked
up her father-in-law's office number. Her
hands trembled, and she redialed three
times before she got the numbers right.

"Please God, help me," she pleaded as she waited for Ed to come on the line.

"Jane? Has something happened?"

He sounded concerned. Was it real? "Why are you doing this?"

"Doing what?"

Was it possible he didn't know? She couldn't hold back the tears. "The custody suit. Having me followed. Am I such a bad mother that you'd be cruel enough to take Sammy from me?"

"Please stop crying," Ed requested. "I can't understand you."

A snuffle escaped as she tried to regain control. "Why did Clarice file for custody of Sammy?"

"What? That's ridiculous," he roared.

"It's true."

"I have to talk to Clarice. I'll call you back."

THIRTEEN

Another day passed with no word from Ed. After getting Sammy to sleep, Jane climbed into bed with paper and pen, making copious lists to share with the attorney. It was late when the phone rang.

"Jane, Ed Holt. Sorry to call now, but I wanted you to know Clarice had a massive heart attack this morning. The doctors don't know if she's going to live."

A gasp slipped out. "What happened?"

"Evidently she's been having problems for a while now. It's a miracle I got there when I did."

Sadness filled Jane. She hadn't wanted anything bad to happen to Sammy's grandmother. "What should we do?"

"I don't know. The prognosis doesn't look good."

"We can pray." Jane suggested the one thing she'd learned worked the best.

"Don't know much about that."

"Talk to God just as you'd talk to a friend," she encouraged him. "Would you like for us to come to Florida?"

"I couldn't ask you to do that."

"No matter what's happened, you're family."

"Maybe having Sammy closer would lift Clarice's spirits when she wakes."

"I'll make the arrangements and let you know. Hopefully we can get a flight out after Sammy's doctor appointment tomorrow."

"Thanks, Jane."

The next morning she and Sammy stopped by the house. Heath was in the family room. "Is Val around?"

"She's in the shower. I thought you were going into Lexington this morning."

"I am, but I needed to tell Val I need time off. Clarice had a massive heart attack yesterday. It doesn't look good."

"I'm sorry."

"Me, too," Jane said. "I didn't want it to be this way."

"When did you plan to go?"

"I booked a noon flight. We'll leave after Sammy sees her doctor. Pray for us, Heath."

"I will. Everyone will."

Because time was at a premium, Jane took the first flight she could get, which also proved to be the most expensive. She hated dipping into her savings but knew she had to do this. One of Ed's employees picked them up at the airport and took them straight to the hospital.

Jane hugged Ed and asked how Clarice was doing. He reported that nothing had changed. They were monitoring her and running tests. He became emotional when Sammy went straight into his arms. The little girl seemed to understand his need for comfort.

With her mother-in-law in the coronary intensive care unit, they spent the time between visits in the waiting area. The long hours gave them plenty of opportunity to talk.

"I'm sorry for the way you've been treated, Jane. Clarice blames you for what Garrett did because she doesn't want to accept our son was selfish. If she dies, it will be yet another wasted life."

Unsure how to respond to her father-in-law's comments, Jane said nothing. For all the years she'd known him, she believed Ed supported his son and wife completely. Now with the custody case pending, she didn't know if she could trust him. "I never meant to upset her."

Ed shook his head. "It wasn't you. I'm sorry I let this go on for so long, but I didn't know how to help Clarice through her misery. The few times I dared say something, she turned that sharp tongue on me. I got tired of fighting and started spending time at the office. I suppose leaving her alone wasn't good either.

"I didn't know what she'd done, Jane. After you called, I went home and confronted her. She told me the truth, and I told her she'd drop this immediately or I'd divorce her and see to it that she never saw Sammy again. We didn't talk again that evening. I left early the next morning, and later that afternoon I started to feel guilty and came home to try to talk some sense into her. When I walked in, I found her slumped over the kitchen island. The phone lay a few inches away. I suppose she tried to call for help."

"I'm sorry, Ed."

"It's not your fault. She had called a friend of hers in Lexington who just happens to be a judge's wife, and the woman talked to her husband. What has happened to my family, Jane?"

Fear nearly took Jane's breath as she considered his revelation. The Holts had money and connections she didn't. She could lose Sammy.

Ed passed Sammy back to her mother and

rested a hand on Jane's shoulder. "I wouldn't have allowed Clarice to take Sammy from you. I talked to the judge. Explained that Clarice has been grieving herself to death and told him we don't want to pursue the custody case."

She hugged her daughter close and said, "We need to stop trying to destroy each other. Garrett is gone, but we can be a family if we try."

"Clarice thought Heath Truelove had proposed. She saw a photo of him giving you a ring."

Jane held out her hand to show him the garnet birthstone. "She should give him more credit. Someone with a name as romantic as Heathcliff would never propose in a parking lot. I admired this ring in the antique store, and he bought it for me as a gift."

He nodded. "I told her she shouldn't assume anything. She's afraid we'll never see Sammy again if you remarry."

"I wouldn't do that," Jane said. "You're her grandparents. Just as Garrett is her father. Telling her what happened to him is going to be hard, but I'll make sure she knows about her father."

"Maybe she doesn't need to know," Ed said. "Tell her he died when she was a baby and leave it at that."

An easy out, Jane thought. She shook her head. "I don't think that's the answer either. She has a right to know."

Ed's sad expression touched her heart. "I'm glad you're thinking about the future. Clarice has been so miserable since his death. She doesn't care about anything. I thought the grief would pass, but she's allowing this to destroy her. Us."

"You haven't . . ." Jane paused, afraid to hear the truth.

"No, but I'm close to calling it quits. I love her, and I loved Garrett, but I won't stop living because he chose to do so. You know how she is. It had to be someone else's fault. Her son would never do something like that."

She had to tell him what she knew. Perhaps learning the truth could help heal this unhappy existence for them all. "There's something I need to share with you."

Jane explained how she'd learned Garrett had cancer. She could see Ed was as shocked by the news as she had been.

"Why wouldn't he tell us?"

"I've asked myself that same question. He took the answer to the grave with him, but based on what the doctor said, I suspect Garrett was in shock. The terminal diagnosis was made only days before he died. The doctor said Garrett could have accidentally killed himself by mixing alcohol and pain-killers."

A glimmer of hope came into the eyes that were so like Garrett's. "Do we pursue this and possibly risk renewed grief?"

"There's not much I can do," Jane told him. "The doctor said to have my lawyer contact him to discuss the matter, but I can't pay another attorney. I'm still paying off Garrett's debts. And now I owe Heath money for the custody case lawyer."

"What kind of debts?" Ed asked.

"Garrett had school loans and credit cards he used a lot."

"Why haven't you said something before? We could have helped."

Jane wanted their independence. She pleaded with Garrett to restrain his spending habits, but he didn't. "They were our obligation."

"I won't have Garrett's irresponsibility stand in the way of you caring for his daughter."

She didn't expect anything of the Holts. "I've been blessed to find a good job, and Val gives me the apartment as part of the package. That helps. I'm paying them down slowly."

Ed drew in a deep breath. "Garrett couldn't even die responsibly. If he'd told the truth and died like a man, his life insurance would have paid."

Jane frowned. "We didn't have life insurance."

"I did. Didn't help you any, though."

His overall attitude seemed so at odds from what she'd always thought about Garrett's father. "I got the impression you supported Garrett as much as Clarice."

"Sure I was proud of him, but it wasn't like he was going to make a living playing football."

"He was good."

"NFL good?"

"We'll never know."

"Clarice got that fool notion that Garrett needed to concentrate on football. One of her friends probably told her he could make a fortune when she bragged about him. I wanted him to work with me during the summers, but it was always football. I thought he'd learn the business and maybe take over when I retired."

Ed ran a successful heating and air-conditioning company in Lexington. He'd made a good profit when he sold the business to one of his employees. He'd started another company in Florida, saying he was too young to retire.

"Why didn't you offer him a job when he dropped out of college?"

"I did. He thought he'd go straight to the top. When I said laborer, he said no thanks. Thought he was too good to work his way up from the bottom like his old man. I don't know where he got the idea that I would hire him to do sales."

"He wasn't very good at it," Jane said, a wry smile touching her face.

"You don't have to tell me. I went to the dealership where he worked, thinking I would put a little business his way, and he thought I'd replace the entire fleet. The boy didn't have a clue how business works."

"He never told me you had offered him a job."

Ed shrugged. "Doesn't surprise me any. You're a good woman, Jane. A good mother, too. I promise you, things are going to change. I won't walk away the next time Clarice starts in on you."

"It's been hard on us all," Jane said, resting her hand on his arm.

He smiled back and patted her hand with his. "I'm so disappointed in Garrett. How can you forgive him?"

"With God's help. I was a believer when I met Garrett, but I allowed my love for him to tempt me into making bad decisions. Lately I've come to realize I need God in my life more than ever."

"Never had any dealings with God."

"You never went to church?"

"We did on Christmas and Easter when we visited my mom's parents."

"I went to church regularly with my parents. I accepted Christ as my Savior when I was ten. I stopped going after I married. I'm praying for Clarice, and my friends and church are praying for her, too."

"My grandmother used to pray a lot," he said thoughtfully.

Jane smiled at that. "Surely you weren't that bad."

Ed grinned for the first time since their arrival. "She believed. She prayed for me, too."

"You don't have to wait for others to pray for you. You have direct access to God. He can make things so much better if you'll just give Him a chance."

A nurse came out into the lobby where they sat. "Mrs. Holt is awake and asking to see you."

He stood and started to follow her. "Wait. This is our daughter and granddaughter. Can they come, too?"

The woman's gaze moved from one to the

other. She nodded.

Jane hesitated. "It might be too much for her."

"No more running away, Jane. Knowing you're here in her time of need will do Clarice a world of good."

Each night Jane took Sammy to the Holt home and put her to bed. Ed gave her a key and often stayed behind in the hospital waiting room. Though Clarice was awake, the doctors weren't sure how much damage had been done to her heart. Although Jane was thankful her condition was no longer critical, Clarice hadn't had a good day, and the situation was still touch and go. The house was quiet when her cell phone rang, and she prepared herself for bad news.

"How's it going?"

"Heath." She breathed his name, relieved to hear his voice. It had been nearly a week since she'd arrived in Florida, and he had called her daily. "I thought it might be the hospital."

"Didn't mean to frighten you. Are you and Sammy okay?"

"We're good. Clarice is really scared."

"I'd think a close call with death would do that to a person."

"She apologized. Then she cried. I told

her they were going to throw me out if she didn't stop. She thanked me for bringing Sammy to see her."

"We've been praying."

"I know," Jane said. "I feel God's presence so strongly. I even witnessed to Ed."

"Good for you."

"How are things there?"

"We went to visit Grandfather Truelove in prison."

Jane knew there had been talk of visiting Mathias Truelove. From what she'd been told, their grandfather had killed a man in a bar fight back when Jacob was just a young man. He blamed his father's addictions to alcohol and gambling for the problems Mathias had caused and was determined that no member of his family would follow the man's example. Val believed her father would never be happy until he forgave his father. "How did it go?"

"I've never seen Dad so upset. I could tell he didn't want to go."

"I'm sure it's difficult for him."

"Even more so when Grandfather talked down to him. When Dad introduced us, he criticized him about our names. Then he started in about us being Christians. Val asked him not to start an argument, and I could see he wanted to say something, but he didn't. He got to her, though. She told Dad that it's sad Grandfather sits in prison day in and day out with no family who cares for him. She said we hadn't given him a reason to want to be a better person."

"How did your dad respond to that?"

"He feels Grandfather got exactly what he deserved. I looked at this old man I didn't remember and yet knew I should respect, and I resented him for what he did to my dad."

Jane understood their plight. It hurt when the people you loved let you down. "That's understandable. You never had an opportunity to bond with him."

"Val says God laid it on her heart to help heal the relationship, but I'm not sure that's possible."

"God will do the healing," Jane said with a level of confidence that surprised her. "He's started the process here between Clarice and me."

"Thanks for reminding me of that. Oh yeah, Val had a meeting at Prestige Designs today. You'll never guess who's behind these incidents with her project. Remember the guy who blamed Val for losing his job at Maddy's office? Derrick Masters. His girlfriend worked for Prestige, and she did all those things for him because Derrick lied to her about the lottery ticket. He made her believe Val cheated him and said she had to help him pay her back. The girlfriend spilled everything, including how Derrick drugged Fancy when he came for the launch party."

"You're kidding." The incidents that had plagued Val's project since the beginning made them all wonder what was going on. She had seen Val's growing frustration over it. Permitting delays, changed work orders, even cancelled supply orders popped up on a regular basis, and now they tied Jacob's accident into the sabotage. Good thing Val had hired security when she did.

"No. Val wouldn't file charges against the woman. She said she was more of a victim than accomplice."

"Will your dad file charges against Derrick Masters?"

"Dad says he won't do anything as long as Derrick stays away from Sheridan Farm."

"Surely he doesn't have the nerve to show his face after what he did."

"I don't know. Look at the mayhem he created with very little effort."

"Tell Val I'm happy things have worked out for her. I have to go," she said a few minutes later. "I need to do a load of laundry before I go to bed. I want to be at the hospital early so Ed can come home and rest."

"Give Sammy a kiss for us. We miss her."

She wondered if he missed her. "I will."

"Jane?" he called softly just before she cut him off. "Hurry home. We miss you, too."

She smiled. "I will. Pray for me."

"You know we will. Pray for us, too."

"You've got a deal, friend."

After their conversation, restlessness enveloped Heath, and he wandered out to the barn. He opened the door to Fancy's stall and smiled when she playfully thrust her nose out. He stroked her gently and fed her a peppermint. He was thankful there were no lingering problems for mother and baby. They had been upset to hear that Fancy had gone out of control and injured their father. They worried about her and the foal she carried.

The sounds of the barn comforted him. As a child, he'd spent lots of time helping his dad with the chores. Mr. Sheridan had praised him and Rom often, saying they were good boys and their father had a right to be proud. Heath always suspected the old man had an investment in their education. Probably in one of the scholarships they'd received. He'd definitely given them a good deal on the small truck they drove back and forth to Lexington.

His thoughts went back to Jane. He hoped she would come home soon. Several times a day he thought of things he wanted to share. He missed Sammy, too. They all did. He didn't want to exist this way.

Heath had prayed Jane would find peace when she told him what she planned to do. She certainly set an example by going to stand by her enemy in the woman's time of need. The women in his life seemed to understand the premise of forgiveness much better than he did.

After securing Fancy's stall, Heath wandered back to the house. He noticed his toy truck on the swing. Setting it on the ground, he settled in the swing and idly thumbed the remote, running the truck in circles.

"Having fun?"

He slid over so Val could sit. "Yeah. Gonna have to talk to the boys about leaving my toys outside though."

She laughed. "You've enjoyed that truck, haven't you?"

"I'm glad Jane insisted that I think about having fun."

"Jane sort of makes you do that, doesn't she?"

"You've noticed it, too?"

"Sure. I laugh more when she's working with us. Those daily cheers of hers are a riot."

After some teasing from them both on her cheerleading youth, Jane had taken to making up cheers to start their day. Her "Rake it to the left, rake it to the right" and the "Trim it high, trim it low" cheers were a real hoot and had them looking forward to what she'd come up with next.

"I enjoy working with her."

He missed those cheers and Jane's playful antics. "Me, too. I couldn't believe it when she insisted on buying me this thing." He hit the control, and Val laughed at the raucous noise it emitted as he ran it around in circles.

"Maybe Jane sees something missing from your life that you don't. God wants you to enjoy life, too, Heath."

"What makes us so driven, Val? Why can't we be free spirits like Jane?"

"Is she really free, Heath?"

"No, I suppose not," he said. "I'm sure there are times when she laughs to keep from crying."

"But she still laughs," Val said. "No matter how bad things get for her, she does everything in her power to lighten everyone else's spirits."

"Do you think that's why she gave me the car?"

"Maybe she thought you needed a little joy in your life. How is she?"

"Seems to be okay. From what she said, it's still touch and go with Clarice. I told her we would continue praying for them. She's proud of herself for witnessing to Ed Holt."

"Me, too. She's come a long way. We've had a few talks, and she's well versed in the Bible. She says it's like riding a bicycle. You never forget."

"That sounds like something she'd say. I miss her and Sammy."

"Did she say when they're coming home?"

"They'll be back for Mom's birthday. I told her about seeing Grandfather. She said selfish men don't mean to be that way. They just can't help themselves."

"She's got a point. We've spent our lives surrounded by generous, loving people. They taught us good life lessons, and we're better people because of them. The situation with Grandfather troubles us all. Just remember only God has the power to change people, but He expects us to forgive."

"We've lived without him all this time. I'm not sure I want him back in our lives now."

"Remember when you said Jane has to forgive Garrett if she wants to get on with her life? What about Daddy?"

"Dad seems okay to me."

"He could be better if he wasn't always struggling with his anger."

"He'll still be angry when Grandfather doesn't change."

"Forgiving someone doesn't mean they don't have the power to hurt us, but it does mean we're more understanding about the things we can't change."

"You should share that with Jane."

"She's better, Heath. I think she's come to grips with the idea that Garrett's death might not have been suicide. She told me she loved him but he's gone and she's ready to move on."

"Move on how?"

"I know for a fact that she'd like a man in her life, a father for Sammy. More kids."

"I'd like to be that man. I suppose I should give serious consideration to my future. Find a job and prepare to support a family. Do you think I'm selfish?"

"Why would you ask that?"

He could tell his question startled her. "Because I've been thinking about myself and what I want out of life instead of my future."

"You've been an industrious student, a good son, and a great brother and friend. All commendable but what does Heath Truelove want out of life?"

"That's easy. A wife who loves me, a family, and a job I love."

"What's kept you from achieving your goals?"

"Personal doubts. You made so many sacrifices to better my life, and I've done nothing for you in return."

"That's not true. I would never have advanced as far with this project without your help."

"Sure you would. You could have hired people and gotten it done faster. Instead you're limping along with me while I recover and wasting your time. I should be out there finding a job like Rom. Not living off you. That money is yours, and somehow I've managed to pocket a big chunk of it for doing nothing. It's not right."

"You don't have anything I didn't willingly give," Val reminded.

"I know, but you deserve more."

"What is this really about, Heath?"

"I've lost my sense of purpose. For years I've had one goal. Get my education and use it to help my family. Lately I'm not helping anyone but myself."

"Have I said or done anything to make you feel this way?"

He hesitated and said, "Well, Opie did say you weren't sure about me doing the garden work."

"Only because I'm afraid you feel like you owe me."

"I do."

"No. You don't. When you and Rom talk about his job, I don't see the excitement that I do when you tell him about the progress in the gardens. I know you only got your master's because you expected to help the family more that way. But guess what, it's okay to be selfish sometimes. Doing what makes you happy is important. Believe me, I've realized it more than ever before since God provided the means to fulfill my dreams.

"Do you think I didn't feel guilty about spending all that money on the farm? I knew we could have found a less expensive place, but I felt there were reasons we needed to stay at Sheridan Farm. I was selfish, too. I didn't want to give up the home I loved. I didn't want Daddy to give up the work he loved. I had my doubts, but when one of the staff tells me how blessed they feel to work for us, God soothes my soul. Did you know Daddy is holding Bible study with some of them?"

"He mentioned it."

"Those things remind me God has a plan for us all. Did you ever think that the changes in our lives were part of the plan He has for us? You feel guilty because you're not using your degree, don't you?"

He nodded.

"But you love what you're doing?"

He nodded again.

"It's okay, Heath. You worked hard for years to please others. Take time for yourself."

"But that's selfish."

"Rom and Opie aren't having problems dealing with the situation."

"Rom got a job, and Opie's using her training."

"Rom's thinking ahead to his future with Stephanie, and Opie's trying to make up her mind. I love you, Heath. I don't have the least bit of doubt that if all the money disappeared tomorrow, you would step up and do what's right. I only want the best for you."

"Just as I want it for you. I want this new venture to be everything you've dreamed of and more."

"With God's help it will be," Val told him. "It's in His hands."

Heath nodded in agreement.

Val leaned her head back against the swing cushions. "Russ should be here soon. He wants to talk."

They had all been shocked to learn who was behind all the incidents that had happened with her project. Any one of which could have put the project at a standstill.

"I'd love to get my hands on Derrick Masters."

"What would you do?" Val asked curiously.

"Though one part of me would love to pummel him into the ground, I don't imagine God or Dad would let that happen."

"How can people be so evil?"

"More selfishness?"

Val frowned. "I feel so guilty for doubting Russ."

"You'll have to make him understand you're sorry. Any idea what he wants to discuss?"

Val shook her head. "I'm thinking he wants to talk about us, but that's probably wishful thinking on my part. Particularly since I've learned he's attending church."

"Life was so much simpler when we were kids."

"These grown-up decisions are difficult."

"Maybe that's why I'm so confused. Jane

says I don't know how to be a kid, but I keep trying to figure out what I want to be when I grow up." Headlights flashed in the distance. "Looks like Russ is here."

"Want to tag along?"

"I wouldn't want to embarrass you while you eat crow."

"You should be a comedian, Heath True-love."

"Gee thanks, yet another option for my career list."

"Don't quit your day job. I need you too much."

"That's good to know."

"Do you doubt you're needed?"

"Jane said a man should have a job and plan for the future. Made me wonder if all women feel that way?"

"I wouldn't want a man who expected me to work and support him."

"I would never expect that of my wife. In fact, I wouldn't want her to have to work at all."

"Don't tell Opie that. She'll be on your case."

He nodded. The entire family knew Opie's feelings on the matter of working women. "I'm not saying she can't work if that's what she wants. Just that I don't want her to have to work to make ends meet. I'd like to provide for my family."

"Most men would," Russ agreed as he walked up on their conversation. "My dad always told us a man's role in life is to provide."

Heath nodded.

"Enjoying this crisp fall weather?" Russ asked.

"It's nice after the summer, but winter comes much too fast," Heath said.

Their stay stretched into weeks. Clarice began to improve, and Jane planned to stay until her release from the hospital. When she saw how weak the woman was, they stayed a few more days to help around the house. Jane cooked and cleaned, and Clarice rested and visited with Sammy. Her daughter's avoidance of her grandmother had lessened with the change in the woman.

The members of the Truelove family called often for progress reports. Jane missed them and longed to go home but knew she had to do this for the Holts.

After putting Sammy down for her nap, Jane asked Clarice if she wanted something to drink. Ed had gone to pick up her prescriptions. "Here you go," Jane said, placing the insulated glass on the table next to

Clarice. "Water with lots of ice and a little lemon."

Clarice studied Jane closely for a few moments longer before thanking her.

"You're welcome."

"No. I mean for what you've done since my attack. You didn't have to bring Sammy to see me. Or be there for Ed when they thought I wouldn't pull through."

"Yes, I did. You're my family, Clarice. No matter what differences we've had, you became my people when I said my wedding vows."

"Some people I've been," she disparaged. "I'm surprised you put up with me as long as you have."

"I got in a few zingers of my own."

"Why did things happen as they did? I knew Garrett would grow up and marry one day. . . ."

"But you never thought it would be a sad little affair like ours?"

"I had such high hopes. I wanted him to accomplish great things. Only problem with that is I never taught him how to do that. I praised him and told him he could do anything he wanted. Then when things turned out badly, to blame him would have been to blame myself. It was easier to put it on you. Ed and I have talked a lot since I got home. I know I have to change or lose you all. I don't know how."

"Have you considered seeking God's help?"

Clarice frowned. "Why would He help me?"

"Because He loves you just as you are."

"Surely not as I am," Clarice said, her doubt-filled tone speaking volumes.

"I thought the same thing until not too long ago. Being around the Trueloves has helped me realize I needed God in my life. Sammy and I attend church, and I've renewed my commitment to God."

"What do you mean, renewed?"

"I accepted Christ as my Savior when I was ten," Jane said. "Then when I moved to Paris and got involved with Garrett, things changed. I still went to church, but I wasn't living a Christian life. I let the need to be popular convince me to make decisions I never should have made."

"You mean the baby?"

The secret she'd carried for years demanded release. Jane took a deep breath and said, "I don't want to hurt you, Clarice, but you need to know it wasn't what you thought. I loved Garrett, but I didn't willingly give him what he wanted. He cajoled and threatened to find someone else, but he never did. My mom warned me to stay clear of temptation, but I thought I could control the situation.

"One night when you and Mr. Holt were out of town, I lied and said I was spending the night with a girlfriend so I could go to an all-night party Garrett had at your house. There was alcohol. I didn't drink, but Garrett did. He got carried away, and when I said no, he didn't listen."

Clarice's face crumpled, and Jane feared she'd gone too far. "That's what Ed said," she whispered. "He was so angry when he learned about the custody case and said our family had already done you enough harm. That's when he told me Garrett all but raped you. Evidently he came to his father when he realized what he'd done. He was afraid your parents would file charges once they learned the truth."

"They don't know," Jane said.

"You let them think badly of you all this time?"

Jane patted her hand. "I blamed myself. If I hadn't gone to the party. If I hadn't lied to my parents. If I hadn't made all those wrong choices. I felt so ashamed. I cried that night. A lot. Garrett didn't know what to do. He sobered up fast, and somehow we made it through the night. I went home the next morning, but I refused to be alone with him again. Then I learned I was pregnant.

"When I told him, Garrett wanted me to get an abortion. I said no. We told my parents, and they wanted me to put the baby up for adoption. I wanted time to consider what was best."

"But that wasn't an option?"

Jane shook her head. "I married Garrett with the intention of making our marriage work."

Clarice's anguished expression tore at Jane's heart. "And I made your life miserable."

"Please don't get upset," Jane said. "It's not good for you. It was my choice. I loved Garrett."

"He loved you, too. I could tell he felt differently about you."

"Did that bother you?"

"You got in the way of my aspirations for my son."

"I had my own aspirations for him."

"Poor Garrett. There was no hope he'd ever live up to our plans for him. I suppose I always knew that, but I had my dreams. I'm sorry for the way I behaved when the baby died."

Tears welled in Jane's eyes. "I loved that baby so much."

"I lost a baby, too. After Garrett. It hurt so much that I thought I'd die, but Ed and Garrett gave me a reason to go on."

Jane knew what God wanted her to do. She had to forgive the Holt family for what they had done to her. "It's in the past, Clarice. I refuse to continue to live like that. God gave us both a wake-up call."

"He did," she agreed. "I've been so afraid. I've become so angry and bitter. Ed threatened to leave me if things don't change. I don't want to be this way. Why can't he understand?"

"You're not dead, Clarice. It's not fair to make the people who love you live with the shadow of a person you've become. You have to love Garrett enough to let go and move forward."

"It's so hard."

"Yes, but we need to go forward for Sammy's sake. She needs her family."

"Can you forgive me for what I did?"

"If you'd taken my child away, I would have hated you forever," Jane said. "I would never have forgiven you."

"I know."

"I want our relationship to be different, Clarice. Ed told me you're afraid I'll marry again and you'll lose Sammy. I promise you that won't happen. My daughter may have three sets of grandparents, but you'll always be there for her. And I will tell her about her daddy."

"What I did was wrong," Clarice said. "You are a good mother, and I had no right implying otherwise. Ed called the judge and explained. He wants to reimburse the Trueloves for the money they've expended for your legal fees."

Unable to speak, Jane nodded.

"I really appreciate the way the Truelove family has looked out for you and Sammy when we haven't. That Heath is a fine young man. He impressed me when we stayed at their home. Told me a few things I didn't want to hear, but I know he was right. Will you marry him?"

"I'd love to, but he seems to be holding back for some reason."

"Why? He obviously cares for you. He took me on about the way I treated you."

"He's a good friend. But he also has definite ideas about what he expects from a woman."

"You're worthy of him, Jane."

"You forget he knows my reputation."

"Tell him what you told me."

"I can't. Not yet. Not until I know for sure that he loves me."

They heard the door open, and Ed called

out that he was home. He walked into the bedroom and handed the pharmacy bag to his wife. "You two okay?"

Clarice squeezed Jane's hand in hers and said, "We're going to be fine."

FOURTEEN

When she decided to return home, Ed drove her and Sammy to the airport. On the way he asked about Heath.

"See Hef?" Sammy asked from the backseat.

"Soon, sweetie." Jane smiled and winked at Ed. "I'd marry him if he'd ask."

Ed looked interested. "Is there a reason you think he won't? I'd say the boy has feelings for you."

"His faith. Heath has very strong beliefs regarding God's intentions for him."

"Don't count yourself out. Love is a powerful motivator, and I'd say Heath loves you and Sammy. Why else would he have done some of the things he has?"

"Because he's like his family. They believe in looking out for people."

"Too bad there aren't more people like that in the world."

Jane agreed.

"Whatever happens, we're behind you all the way," Ed said. "I know you have plans for the future, and I want to help in every way possible. I hope you'll let me do that."

"I thank you for that. I want to do right by Sammy, and I think I'm in the best place for now. I'm learning a lot about myself and what I'm capable of doing."

"Starting at the bottom?" he asked with a smile.

Jane thought about what he'd said about Garrett. "Definitely."

"It's best to build a secure foundation in life. Helps you keep the other things in the right perspective."

She insisted he drop them off at the gate so he could get back to Clarice as soon as possible. "Thank you for all you've done. Knowing the custody issue is resolved takes away a major burden."

"I'm sorry it happened in the first place. Thank you for all you've done for Clarice and me. I think maybe we're on the right track now. In fact she mentioned that she'd like to attend church when she's able to get out again."

That pleased Jane a great deal. "Will you let me know how it goes?"

He nodded. "We'll be in close contact. I'll

let you know how it turns out with Garrett, too."

Ed lifted their luggage out of the trunk and then unstrapped Sammy from the child seat. He hugged them both and waved good-bye before driving away.

A lot had happened in her absence. She was happy for Val when she learned she and Russ were dating with the intention of one day becoming man and wife.

She returned just in time for Cindy True-love's birthday celebration. Jane gladly tackled her first job assignment of helping sort out plans for the two parties planned to celebrate the day for the woman who meant so much to her and Sammy. The first was a community event involving family, friends, and their church. The second was a private affair for family and friends.

As she worked with Heath, Jane considered what she must do. She couldn't be in his presence and not have his love. They discussed what had happened in Florida and how Ed planned to hire an attorney to pursue the matter of Garrett's death certificate. Jane didn't tell him her father-in-law had insisted on paying off all of Garrett's debts and she had returned to Paris with a lighter load. He had been surprised when she handed him the Holts' check reimbursing the legal fees he'd incurred with interest. She did tell him she was ready to move on with her future.

"Can you do that if you're still grieving for Garrett?"

Jane stopped filling balloons with helium and said, "Garrett is dead, Heath. I was a child when I fell in love with him. Innocent and trusting but what I didn't realize was that he was a child, too. We made decisions that changed the course of our lives, believing no one had a right to tell us what to do. Our parents, even our child, suffered from those choices. I'm a wiser woman. I understand that we can't always have everything we want in life."

"What do you mean, everything?" Heath asked.

"Sometimes the people we love don't love us back."

"Why would you say that?"

"I know you'd never consider me wife material."

Heath looked puzzled, and Jane had said far more than she intended. Maybe it would be best if she and Sammy moved on. Both of them would be hurt if they stayed around and Heath married someone else. "I have to go. Val's waiting for me in the office. She said something about running into Paris to pick up supplies. And I need to get Cindy's gift."

"Jane?" Heath called after her.

What did she mean? he wondered as he watched her escape to the house. *"The people we love don't love us back."* That sounded almost as if . . . Was it possible that she was trying to tell him she loved him?

She seemed different since she'd learned that Garrett's death was possibly accidental, but that only made him fear she still loved her husband. She'd said others had disappointed her. Maybe Jane meant her parents? Even her in-laws. Heath wished he knew for sure.

"God, I love Jane and I feel like she's the one You intend for me, but I need to know she's over Garrett and ready to serve You wholeheartedly. Give us answers, and if it's Your will, grant us this happiness that love and a lifetime of commitment to You would provide."

"Is that a thundercloud over your head?" Val asked when Jane stepped into the office.

"Men can be so dense."

"All men? Or one in particular?"

Disgusted, Jane said, "Heath. I know I'm

not wife material in his eyes. I tried to tell him I understood. . . ."

"Why would you think that?" Val interrupted.

"Heath has shared certain expectations regarding the woman he marries. He said she will be pure of heart, and since he's saving himself for marriage, I'm sure she'll be pure in other ways as well."

"I don't believe that's Heath's reason."

"Then what is?" Frustrated, Jane paused and said, "I'm sorry. I shouldn't have asked you that."

"I know how you feel," Val told her. "I love Russ, and when I felt like there was no hope of a future together, it tore me up inside even though I knew I made the right decision. I'm happy God made it possible for us, but I had my doubts it would ever happen."

Her friend had shared her turmoil over loving a man she couldn't have. "And if it's God's will, things will work out for me."

"You can be sure that God will put the right man in your life. Pray, Jane. Ask God for what you want."

"I do, Val. It's hard when you love someone, though."

"Very hard but know that even if it doesn't happen exactly like you want, that can be an answer to a prayer, too."

"Do you love Jane?"

Val's blunt question threw Heath off guard. Jane must have said something after their conversation before the party.

"Yes."

Val frowned. "Why does she think she doesn't stand a chance with you?"

"I don't have a clue."

"Have you told her how you feel?"

He shook his head. "I'm waiting for answers."

"Prayers?"

Heath nodded. "I have to be sure."

Val eyed him speculatively. "You doubt she loves you?"

"I'm not sure she's over Garrett. She's still so angry."

"Do you feel she isn't entitled?"

"I believe any hope for happiness she might have depends on her choosing to forgive. This latest revelation about his cancer has helped her. Once she got over the shock, she seemed relieved."

"What do you feel that God is telling you?"

"I'm trying to wait on His guidance. The doubts come when I remember that I wasn't enough for her in her youth. She needed excitement then. What if that happens in the future?"

"Jane experimented with popularity, and it came up lacking. If you're willing, you can provide the excitement along with the stability she craves."

"I know that she's the one, but grieving is a process. She has to be ready for the future before she moves on."

"She claims that's what she's doing."

"She's trying, but some of the things she does and says make me wonder if she's as far along as she thinks," Heath said. "What do you think she'll do?"

"I know what I'd do. I should say, did. When I realized how I felt about Russ, I offered to be his friend, and he disappeared from my life."

His forehead creased. "You think she'll offer to become my friend?"

Val shook her head. "I don't see Jane as the type to stick around when she feels she's not wanted."

Val left, and Heath thought about what she'd told him. She was right. He needed to talk to Jane. To understand what she'd been trying to tell him.

"Take a walk with me?" he requested later that afternoon. He'd exchanged the cast for an orthopedic boot while she'd been gone. He moved slowly, but at least he moved without crutches.

Jane shrugged. They'd worked hard all day, but she supposed the exercise couldn't hurt. They strolled through the horse barns, checking out the new horses the farm had acquired.

"Beautiful animals," Jane said.

"Expensive but they'll pay for themselves in a very short time."

After leaving the barn, they took a circuitous route and ended up in the Oriental garden. "This is my favorite garden," Heath said, patting the bench next to him.

Jane sat down. "I like the English garden best."

"I'm surprised. It's so structured. I think of you as a free-spirited kind of girl."

"Sometimes structure can be a good thing."

He'd thought about the situation all afternoon and concluded that it was time to take action. He couldn't risk losing her because he was too afraid to step out on faith and trust God to make things work for them. "Are you thinking of leaving Sheridan Farm?"

She tensed as if shocked by his question.

"I've considered it."

"Can I ask why?"

She plucked a dying leaf from a nearby plant and shredded it with her fingers. "You really need to ask?"

"I suppose not. I care for you, Jane. A great deal. There are things I'm uncertain about, but I know that for sure. Val reminded me today how she distanced herself from Russ because she knew God wanted differently for them. Russ distanced himself from her because he couldn't bear being near her when they didn't have a future. He didn't understand why she had to make that choice. They had a very tough time."

"I know. Val told me."

"Would you do the same for me?"

Jane couldn't look him in the eye. "I care for you, too," she admitted, her head down as she spoke the words. "These past few months have opened my eyes to so much. I've made mistakes. I've confessed my sins to God, and He's forgiven me. I'm thankful for that. I truly believe that if I allow God to control my future, it will be brighter and better than anything I ever considered."

"I'm confused, too, Jane. I love you and can't tell you how happy I am that you've given your life over to God. But I'm afraid you're still grieving for Garrett."

"Why would you think that?" she demanded, sitting up and looking at him. After a brief silence, she said, "I suppose it does seem that way. I don't know if what I feel is grief or anger for what he did to us."

"You two had a lot of unresolved issues. Do you think your marriage would have survived if he were still alive?"

"I made a commitment," she said. "I would have done everything possible to keep us together, but I doubt Garrett would have done the same. Whatever his reasons for being attracted to me, Garrett knew I wasn't like the other girls. He would have left me for someone more exciting eventually."

"I doubt he'd find anyone more exciting," Heath said. How could she not see that about herself?

"I was a child. Immature and thought I was invincible."

Then Jane shared the truth of her first experience with Garrett. Emotions like he'd never known washed over him. The desire to protect her from future hurt was foremost in his heart.

"I can't believe he did that to you."

"You walked away from temptation, but if you'd stayed that night, don't you think things would have gotten out of control?"

"I know they would have."

"Every time Garrett threatened to find someone else, I believed he would. My insecurities precipitated an action that made me a woman before my time. Mistake or not, I couldn't go back. I was so ashamed. Knowing I'd disappointed God only made it worse."

"Is that why you said I don't consider you wife material?"

"Yes. And because you . . ."

"I saved myself for the woman God intended, and I'm pretty sure that woman is you. You don't have to worry about the one you love loving you back. Working so closely with you with my doubts has been difficult, but I couldn't bear not having you close either. I love you."

"Are you sure?"

He smiled and touched her cheek gently. "Very much so. I've loved you from afar for years, but I never considered there was any hope of us becoming a couple."

"Maybe not then," she admitted. "But things changed when you came back into my life. There's so much about you that I admire and love."

"So where do we go from here?"

"Where do you want to go?"

"I want to get to know Jane Kendrick Holt better. I'd like to be 100 percent sure that we're ready for our future. Once we're sure, I want to settle down and raise a family."

"What you see is what you get," she warned. "I've renewed my relationship with Christ, but I'm still human. I've been a wife and mother, and I can't go back to the innocence you once told me you wanted in your future bride. But I can promise to commit completely to you, and there's nothing in life I'd love more than to be your wife and the mother of your children."

"You agree that we need to take our time and do this right?"

She nodded. "I jumped in over my head when I was just a child and nearly drowned in all that misery I brought upon myself. I want to go into this relationship with my eyes open and my heart ready to receive all the love you have to offer. I need you to feel the same."

FIFTEEN

November turned into December, and if possible, Heath felt as if every day of his life got better and better. He and Jane had their alone times, but they also spent a lot of time with Sammy. Forming a bond with her was important to their future. He loved Sammy and wanted them both to know he would never put her aside for another child.

The future seemed to be constantly on his mind. If he intended to have a family, he needed to think about finding a job. He had the money Val had given him for graduation, but how could he utilize it successfully to provide for all their needs? The most logical choice was to find a position that paid him a regular salary with benefits.

Of course that presented the probability of leaving Paris, which created yet another problem. He didn't want a long-distance relationship. He'd spent too much time apart from Jane. He knew she'd probably move to wherever he went, but she was happy living and working at the farm. Maybe they could discuss it after the New Year and come to some sort of agreement.

Hand in hand, they strolled through the antique store. "Val's already talking about how we'll decorate the house," Jane said. "She plans to have a big party. Sammy won't know what to think with so many Christmas celebrations."

The lack of space in their old house had limited the decorating. This year would be a first in many ways. "Our family has great plans for your daughter."

"Just remember our apartment is not very large."

"Then we'll have to give her a big play-house."

She looked at him askance.

"Just kidding. No one's mentioned a playhouse," Heath said. "At least not yet."

Jane found herself looking forward to the holidays more than she had in years. Except for a couple of small weddings in the downstairs portion of the house, Your Wedding Place had pretty much gone on hold until spring. Jane didn't mind much since the focus shifted to decorating the house.

They cut tons of boxwood and holly from

the gardens, and Cindy had taught them how to turn it into wreaths and garlands. The green garland combined with ribbons and miniature white lights made an impressive display both on the outside and inside of the house.

They saved the tree for last, and Val spent days coming up with the perfect decorations for the massive evergreen that would sit in the drawing room. She wanted smaller trees throughout the house and kept Jane busy coming up with ideas. The one tree that stayed the same was the family tree in the den. Those decorations were a collection of things the Truelove children had made over the years, and there was a great deal of laughter as they decorated the tree. Jane was touched when Cindy and Sammy made dough ornaments for them to include on the tree.

They found boxes of old decorations left behind by the Sheridans' son and enjoyed their beauty. "Val feels guilty over using these," Jane told Heath as they admired the glass ball ornaments.

"William obviously didn't want them."

"She says they're treasures."

"You know what they say about trash and treasure. Have you decorated your tree yet?"

"We have a little tree with nonbreakable

ornaments. I've warned Sammy not to touch anything in here."

Heath grinned. "I'm sure she'll heed your warning when one of these beautiful ornaments calls her name."

"That's why these rooms are off-limits without adult supervision. I can't afford to replace them."

"They were free, remember?"

She reached for another box. "Mrs. Sheridan liked variety. I've never seen so much stuff."

"They hosted lots of parties. I'm sure she liked to vary her decorations."

"Did you see the carousel horses? Val has those on the tree in her office."

Heath shifted the boxes out of the way and sat down next to her on the sofa. "What should I get Sammy for Christmas? I tried thinking like a two-year-old, but I came up blank."

"She loves Horsie. You did good with that."

"What about a rocking horse? One of those stuffed ones that resembles the real thing."

"As long as we don't have to feed and comb it, I'm sure she'd love one."

"Is that a hint not to buy her a pony?"

Jane dropped the handful of ornament

hooks she was trying to separate into the box. "I know your family really wants her to have one, but she needs to wait until she's old enough to care for a pet."

"I suppose puppies and kittens are off-limits, too?"

"Please, Heath, there are days when one little girl nearly stretches me to the limit. She can play with the animals you already have."

"Okay, I'll put the word out."

"Thanks."

"What about you? What would you like?"

"Peace and goodwill. This will be the first year Sammy really knows what's going on, and seeing her enjoy herself is really all I want. I pray her grandparents feel the same."

"Any word on Clarice?"

"She's trying. She really is," Jane said earnestly. "She wanted to buy Sammy a Christmas dress and actually called to ask my opinion."

"She's shopping?"

"From catalogs."

"Sounds like a step in the right direction."

"It's a giant leap," Jane said. "In all the years I've known her, Clarice has never been interested in my opinion on anything."

"Sounds like you might get your Christmas wish this year. So you'll be staying with them for a few days before and heading for your parents' afterward?"

"Val gave me two weeks' vacation. We'll see the Holts and come home for Christmas."

"Home?"

"Here at the farm. I want Sammy to sleep in her bed on Christmas Eve. We'll leave for Colorado the day after Christmas."

"You'll be exhausted."

"I know. I'd love to stay home, but if the family won't or can't come to us, we have to go there."

"At least Sammy will get to be in the church Christmas program."

Jane thought about her budding starlet and chuckled. "I have no idea what she'll come out with onstage. They tried her costume on her last night, and she didn't want to take it off. Maybe you should get her some dress-up outfits. Thank goodness, she's not in the live nativity. Though I'm still not sure why I let you talk me into that."

"Because you love the Lord and want to do good works in His name."

"I do," Jane agreed. Secretly she looked forward to dressing as Mary and kneeling next to Baby Jesus with Heath at her side as Joseph.

"Don't your parents want you there for Christmas?"

"Mom and I usually end up arguing. She treats me like a child and questions my judgment. I'd just as soon not hear it through the holidays."

"How do you plan to handle that?"

"With lots of prayer. I'm hoping she's seen enough of a change in our recent conversations to know that I'm trying. She has to trust me, too."

"What happens if she doesn't?"

"I've got it under control." She stuck out her tongue at him. "See the teeth marks?"

Heath grinned. "Don't bite too hard, or talking back won't be a problem."

"I always feel like I have to defend myself."

"You'll see it differently when Sammy starts telling you no," Heath said.

"She already does."

"And it's cute now, but she needs to know you mean business. Sorry. I shouldn't tell you how to parent."

Jane smiled at him. "I know I let her get away with too much, but she's so little and so cute."

"She is that. Perhaps you should consider talking openly about the past with your mother."

"You mean tell her what happened that

night?" Jane couldn't help but wonder how her mother would react to that news after all this time. Jane had a feeling her mom would be even more upset because she hadn't told them the truth.

"That and what you want from the future."

"I want the same things I wanted back then. Except now my hopes center around Sammy's needs more than my own. I suppose in a way I understand Mom's feelings. When she questions my choices, she questions herself. I'm sure she thinks if she'd prepared me better I wouldn't have made mistakes."

Heath shook his head. "Mistakes aren't something we can avoid. What do you think about me going with you to visit your parents?"

Jane appeared startled. "Why would you want to?"

"I think it's time I met them, and they won't come here. I thought I'd fly up for the last day of your visit and return home with you and Sammy."

"No. Let's go together. You do need to get to know them, and they need to know you."

SIXTEEN

When the remote control car bounced off her leg, Jane looked up to find Heath leaning against the door frame, grinning at her.

"Hey, I'm still learning how to drive the thing. Merry Christmas!"

Jane and Sammy had returned home from Florida in plenty of time to join the Truelove family's Christmas Eve celebration. After a delicious traditional dinner, they moved the celebration to the drawing room.

A gift rested in the body of the toy truck. The beautifully wrapped and beribboned package reeked of an elegant store's salesperson's abilities.

"You shouldn't have," she said, all the while ripping away the paper. Jane tried not to show her disappointment when the gift turned out to be a box of chocolates. "Thank you. I love them."

Heath crossed the room and sat next to

her on the love seat. "Aren't you going to share?"

She held the unopened box out to him.

He pushed it back into her hands. "You have to take the first piece."

Jane noticed the way everyone in the room watched them as she pulled the outer wrapping off the box and lifted the lid. Dumbfounded, she stared down at the velvet bed stuffed where a piece of candy had previously rested. The round solitaire diamond with smaller diamonds around the band glittered against the chocolate and was the most beautiful thing she'd ever seen.

"Hope you don't mind that I already ate a piece," Heath said with a big grin. "Do you like it?"

"I love it."

He pulled the ring from the box and dropped to one knee right there in front of his entire family and asked, "Jane Kendrick Holt, will you do me the honor of becoming my wife?"

"Oh yes!" she cried, flinging her arms around his neck. "I thought you'd never ask."

He slid the ring on her finger, and laughter filled the room as the others came over to offer their congratulations.

"I can't believe you did this," Jane said

later when he walked them home. Sammy slept against Heath's shoulder, and he held Jane's hand in his.

"I wanted you to understand just how serious I am."

"Does this mean you're ready to set a date?" She wanted him to say yes.

"Not right away. I still have to make provisions for supporting you and Sammy. I have to find a job and . . ."

"You have a job," she protested. "One you enjoy. I see no reason for you to give it up."

"I have to provide for my family."

"You will. We can work together with Val on her project."

"The pavilion is nearly finished."

"It needs to be landscaped. I know you have great plans for that. Then there's the other structure she plans. And all those new gardens. Why not see them through?"

"This project could go on for years."

"And I'm sure Val would be willing to tell everyone what a tremendous job you've done. You don't have to take a stodgy office job if that's not what you want. Find a way to use your degree to do something you enjoy. Life is too short to be miserable because that's what you think other people expect."

"Do you want to live in a garage apartment and not have the things you deserve because your husband is following his dream?"

Jane held up her hand. The porch light reflected off the beautiful ring. "Accepting this gives me responsibility as well. I'd rather you be happy and content than have things I don't need. Don't make the sacrifice for me, Heath. I don't want it."

He carried Sammy in and put her to bed, pausing long enough to kiss Jane good night before he left for home. The unresolved situation caused her to lose sleep that night, and she determined to track Heath down the following morning and continue the discussion. Then again, they were scheduled to fly to Colorado in two days. There would be plenty of time to discuss it on the plane.

And discuss it they did. Jane remained resolute in her determination that she didn't care what he did so long as he was happy doing it.

She hadn't mentioned their engagement to her parents, and they were shocked when she called to ask if there was room for Heath.

"What's going on, Jane? You're not living with him, are you? I won't have you sharing a bedroom in my home."

Jane almost laughed at her mother's comments. "No, Mother. It's not that type of relationship. I suppose you could say we're considering a future together."

"Considering? You either are or aren't, Jane."

"Okay. He's asked me to marry him, and I said yes. I wanted to surprise you."

Her mother didn't say anything.

"Mom?"

"I want to be happy for you, Jane. It's just that you've . . . well, you haven't always made the best choices."

"Just give me a chance, Mom. And you'll like Heath. I promise."

"When will you be arriving?"

SEVENTEEN

"Ready?"

Tears of joy filled her eyes as Jane nodded. In minutes she would become Mrs. Heath Truelove, and the thought filled her with extreme joy. The last few months had been better than Jane could have imagined.

She truly had witnessed the miracle of Christmas this year. The Holts, the Trueloves, even her parents had made the holiday memorable in ways she'd never forget. Next to Heath's proposal, the best gifts she'd gotten for Christmas were the pleasurable time spent with everyone and hearing her mother say she'd chosen wisely. There was no question her dad liked Heath. They had clicked immediately. Her father was very impressed with Heath's business acumen and told Jane he would go far in life.

Heath hadn't given up on his quest to convince Jane to talk with her mother. While the men helped Sammy build a snowman in the front yard, they sat in the living room and talked. After telling the story she'd kept secret for all those years, Jane explained that she accepted complete responsibility for what had happened. Tears fell as her mother apologized for pushing her into marriage and deserting her when she needed her most.

Jane told her parents that she'd found her way back to the Lord because of Heath and the Trueloves, and she hoped never to get lost again. They expressed their gratitude for all he and his family had done for her and Sammy.

When Russ proposed to Val on Valentine's Day, Jane was so happy for her friend. Every day it seemed as if Val came up with some new plan for her wedding, and Jane wished she and Heath could set the date and move forward with their lives. Val and Russ set the date for their June wedding and hired Maddy as their wedding planner. Opie finally overcame the bronchitis and bout of pneumonia that had plagued her throughout the winter and planned to cater the event from the pavilion kitchen.

They continued working with Val. Heath had plans in place for the pavilion, and they waited for a break in the weather to start work on the landscape. She knew Heath still had doubts about providing for their future. Jane wished he understood that she didn't care what he did as long as he was content.

She'd never forget the moment they chose their wedding date. The sun had finally broken through on the late March morning, and they watched from their seats on the steps as the contractors laid patio stones around the pavilion.

"You're going to have a spectacular wedding locale," Jane said.

Val nodded. "Russ and I were talking, and he suggested I throw this out there to you. We wondered if you would like to get married on the same day."

Jane looked expectantly at Heath.

He shrugged and said, "Okay with me."

Just that easily they had joined in the excitement of planning a wedding. At first Jane had been apprehensive that her simple wedding would conflict with Val's elaborate plans, but in the end it had all worked out. The rehearsal last night had gone perfectly, and Jane knew this time her wedding memories would be wonderful.

"Don't cry," her father said, using his handkerchief to dab away the tears. "Your mom will be upset if you have raccoon eyes in your wedding pictures."

She managed a misty smile as she assured

him her mascara was waterproof. At times the road to forgiveness became a long journey, but Jane knew that with God's help she had arrived at her final destination.

"Where is she?"

"She wanted you to have the earrings she wore on our wedding day. She left them in our bedroom at the house. I can't get over how scatterbrained she's been this week."

Jane smiled at him, and he squeezed the hands he held in his.

"You're a beautiful bride," James Kendrick said. "This is what I wanted for you, Jane. I was so disappointed when you and Garrett were married in that civil ceremony."

"I know, Daddy. I'm sorry."

"I love you, Jane. I only want the best for you. Your mother and I know we played a role in those choices you made. We should have been less trusting and more involved in your life. We realize we depended on you to make decisions you weren't old enough to make."

"You'd only have known what I wanted you to know. I hid the truth. I knew better, but I let myself get into a situation that changed my life. I stood by my decisions, though."

"You did, and I'm proud of you and what

you've accomplished. God has blessed you with a good man who loves you and Sammy. Heath will be a good provider."

Jane had no doubt about that. Heath finally got it when her dad told him the same thing after the rehearsal dinner last night. The Trueloves were very supportive and even suggested they move into the old family home. When they agreed, Val insisted on doing a few upgrades, and Jane looked forward to raising their family in the house where Heath had grown up.

When she said yes to Heath's proposal, Jane never considered a formal wedding. She thought second marriages should be low-key. Heath had other ideas. He insisted that with a sister in the wedding business they would never get away with simple. Jane knew it wasn't what he wanted anyway. As romantic as his name, Heathcliff Truelove wanted their minister to marry them in the sight of God and all their family and friends.

When she tried to get out of buying a wedding dress, the female members of the Truelove family and her mother banded together and took her shopping.

Someone had once told her that when you put on *the* dress you knew, and she certainly had. Simple but classy, the lace illusion halter followed her form in a fitted style with a swiss dot tulle overlay. The Watteau train attached to the top of the gown and trailed out behind her. A stylist had done her hair at the house that morning, and it was bigger than usual to support the tiara the Truelove women had insisted she must wear.

"Whew," Wendy Kendrick declared as she raced from the stairway. "Will you wear these?"

Jane looked at the earrings her mother placed in her hand. She remembered them from childhood. They had always intrigued her, but her mother had warned her they weren't toys. The fact that she trusted Jane with them now spoke volumes. She quickly removed the earrings she wore and replaced them with her mother's diamond drop earrings. Wendy dropped the others into her clutch purse.

"Perfect." Her mother kissed her cheek. "I love you, Jane."

"I love you, too, Mom."

They rode up to the pavilion's main floor together. An usher proffered his arm, and her mother winked playfully. Jane couldn't get over the difference in her since their conversation at Christmas. Wendy Kendrick took a moment to speak to Sammy before being escorted down the aisle.

Emotion surged anew at the sight of Sammy wandering aimlessly down the aisle, tossing the occasional flower as she visited with people she knew. At the rate her daughter moved, the wedding wouldn't start for hours. After a few minutes, Cindy gestured, and Sammy ran the rest of the way and climbed into her lap.

When Wendell, Russ's brother, played the first strains of Pachelbel's Canon in D on the baby grand piano, she and her father took the first step of the rest of her life.

As the woman he loved walked toward him, Heath could only smile and thank God for the miracle he had been given. Never in all his life had he ever considered that Jane would one day become his wife. Always beautiful, today she came to him wearing a white wedding gown. When she argued that she shouldn't wear white, Heath reminded her that God had washed her as white as snow. She'd cried when he told her that, admitting she had feared she could never be the pure woman he sought.

She smiled at the Holts, who sat in the pew behind her mother. Heath was glad they accepted him as a stepfather for their grandchild. Jane paused to hand roses to Clarice, her mother, and then his mother to symbolize the connection of their family before she stepped before him.

"Who gives this woman in marriage?"

Her father responded, placing her hand in his. Jane smiled her glorious smile, and Heath knew nothing else mattered as long as they had each other. In their lifetime, careers would change, children would grow up and leave home, but love would sustain them. Their future would be about choices. Some good, some bad, but every decision, just as those they'd made in the past, would make them the people God wanted them to be. Heath had no doubt God had chosen Jane to be his wife and knew that, because he had listened and allowed Him to choose, their love would prosper and bear fruit in a marriage that would last a lifetime.

ABOUT THE AUTHOR

Terry Fowler is a native Tarheel who loves calling coastal North Carolina home. Single, she works full-time and is active in her small church. Her greatest pleasure comes from the way God has used her writing to share His message. Her hobbies include gardening, crafts, and genealogical research. Terry invites everyone to visit her Web site at terryfowler.net.

The employees of Thorndike Press hope you have enjoyed this Large Print book. All our Thorndike, Wheeler, and Kennebec Large Print titles are designed for easy reading, and all our books are made to last. Other Thorndike Press Large Print books are available at your library, through selected bookstores, or directly from us.

For information about titles, please call:
 (800) 223-1244

or visit our Web site at:
 http://gale.cengage.com/thorndike

To share your comments, please write:
 Publisher
 Thorndike Press
 10 Water St., Suite 310
 Waterville, ME 04901

Uncle Zeb had offered them a finished room over his garage when they lived in Boston.

They hadn't experienced a traditional college lifestyle, but they had been together in a way. Heath figured this separation was good preparation for the future when Rom married Stephanie and they became permanently separated. He missed his twin and wondered if Rom felt the same way. "Want me to help with the move or work in the garden?"

"The new bride requested the English garden. Other than a few requested changes, it's ready, so let's get moved and settled. Once that's out of the way, we can get back to work on the business."

Early the following morning they loaded boxes into the truck and drove over to the mansion. Cindy had taken the younger kids into town for school supplies and doctor appointments. She'd offered to take Sammy, but Jane knew the little girl would tire too soon and give them a hard time.

She settled Sammy in the office with her books and toys but had her doubts about her daughter's staying power. Jane carried her box upstairs and checked in on the trip down. Sammy had abandoned the items in

DATE DUE

070713		
MAR 14 2015		
April 6, 2015		
DEC 2 0 2018		
APR 2 9 2019		
APR 2 9 2019		